George the Dragon

A fantasy novella
By Braeden Mullen

Table of contents

Chapter 1 - Daydreams

The dragon spread its wings showing its majesty to the armies laid before it, a challenge for any great beast, but this was no mere dragon. It was a grand member of its race, mighty, powerful and large. It opened its maw to unleash the torrent of power stored within it, obliterating the Lich Lord's army in seconds.

Or that's what it looked like to George. He laid on the grass inspecting the clouds, and when he squinted his eyes at just the right angle it looked like a dragon. That cloud there looked like an evil wizard, so it worked in his mind.

It was an odd day, he had finished all his chores, it was a warm fall day and the festival would start soon. George looked down the hill at the cozy little farming village where nothing exciting ever happened.

Except George knew a secret. In the evening when the villagers all gathered together a strange shadow would fly overhead in the clouds. At first he had thought it was his wild imagination, but after a few weeks he had grown suspicious. It was too large to be a bird, and it wasn't one of the king's flying machines.

Which left him with an idea of what it could be. A dragon stopping by the village lake for a quick drink. It made sense, the king had several dragon's under his employment to ferry messages to the distant fortresses guarding the borders. Sleepy Hollow was a little town at just the right route from the capital to the fort.

George had a smile on his face and a wild look in his eyes. Tonight while everyone was distracted by the games and food at the festival he would quietly sneak away to meet the dragon. There were tales from the travelling bards that if you met a dragon in its real form you could make a wish.

George watched a crow circle overhead and he immediately knew what he would wish for. To be a dragon of course!

The walk down the hill and into the forest scared many people of Sleepy Hollow, they would jump at the smallest sounds in the woods. George might have been only eight, but he was the bravest boy in town. He wasn't scared of some wild critter looking for berries.

In the bushes behind him something stepped on a branch. The sharp crack of breaking dried wood caused him to jump away and look back. George put his hands on his hips as he saw the strange pudgy animal look at him with its black rimmed eyes.

"Bandit!" George said irritably. "What did I say about sneaking up on me?"

The raccoon cackled as it sat on its back feet rubbing its little paws together. The raccoon had fallen ill last year and George had brought it old blankets and scraps of food to help it recover. Ever since Bandit had become his special pal, who would bring him fallen shiny things in exchange for food.

George crouched down to be on eye level with Bandit and took out a strip of dried meat from his pocket. "Alright Bandit, what do you have to trade?"

Bandit had a tiny pouch on a drawstring around his neck and from it he produced a gold coin. George's eyes widened at seeing the golden disc, it was worth more than his family farm made in a month. They could purchase another cow with the single coin.

"Want to trade, Bandit?" George asked, offering the strip of meat.

Either Bandit was playing hardball or the raccoon knew about money because the critter bared his teeth and put the coin back into the pouch. George knew his family could use the money more than a raccoon so to sweeten the deal he added five dried raisins.

Bandit loved raisins and the smart little raccoon gave up the coin for his favourite snack. George watched with amazement as the raccoon slapped the golden disc into his hand and he put the food out in front of the raccoon finalizing the exchange.

First the raisins, then the meat vanished into the sharp toothed maw of the raccoon and the happy critter slapped his growing belly. With the winter on the horizon George felt Bandit had enough fat on him to last two winters. Which was good because last winter Ma had caught him sneaking out raisins and it was hard to convince her that he needed them for the tight fisted business raccoon.

George ruffled up Bandit's fur and the raccoon lightly slapped away his hand making an irritable noise. Bandit had never harmed him so he wasn't scared of his teeth, it was just to let him know Bandit had places to be. The raccoon vanished into the bushes and the last George saw of him was of his tail wagging.

The rest of the forest walk was quiet with only the occasional caw of a crow above him. Perhaps the birds had seen the valuable coin vanish into the young boy's pocket and watched in case it fell. George frowned and kept a hand on his side ensuring the coin was still there. The heavy weight and smooth shape of the coin reassured him, and the boy broke into a light skip the rest of the way home.

His house was at the outskirts of town and as George walked by the wooden fence the cows greeted him with mighty moos. As he passed by them he took a moment to scratch each under the chin and called them by name.

"Bessie, Margret, Hannah, Liz, Tiffy, how's it going Ash?"

The cows mooed after their names were called and George was happy to see all of them were present and accounted for. If they had jumped the fence when he was supposed to be watching them his Ma would have freaked out for sure.

"George!" Ma called from the house. She peered from the steps out into the field. "Where is that boy?"

"Hi Ma!" George said, running up to her. "When I went to check on the far fence you won't believe what I managed to trade for with Bandit today."

Ma gave him a skeptical look as she folded her arms. "Bandit, the magical raccoon Bandit?"

"Ma don't be silly. He's just a normal raccoon," George said. He then flashed the coin to her. "For five raisins and a piece of jerky I got this."

Ma pulled at her hair and quickly looked around. No one else was there but the two of them and the cows. Ma took the coin and stuffed it into her apron so quickly George didn't even have time to see her take it from him.

"George, this is a lot of money. Where did you get it?" Ma asked quietly.

"I'm being honest Ma, Bandit finds all kinds of shiny things to trade. Come with me, I'll show you," George said.

As George took her to his room they passed the dinner table where all his siblings sat. They had their shoes on and were talking about all the prizes they would win at the town fair. George considered telling them about the dragon and to see if they wanted to come with him but they never believed him when he talked about it before.

George made up his mind, he would go see the dragon and they could enjoy the fair. His brother Paul and him were the best at ball games in the village which meant his family was sure to win some big prizes tonight.

Finally reaching his room George took Ma to his bed and got the box underneath it. As he undid the clasps on the box he smirked wondering how Ma was going to react. The box opened and he proudly presented his treasure trove to Ma.

"George, what is all this junk?" Ma asked, holding a hand to her head. "Is this all from the raccoon?"

"Of course Ma! There's all kinds of buttons, buckles and rings here," George said, taking time to show her each treasure.

"This is Mrs. Gill's lost wedding ring, this is a silver button from the mayor's coat. George, what are people going to think?" Ma asked.

"I…well Bandit found them," George said.

"George, we are going to have to find a way to return all this," Ma said. She took out the gold coin and frowned. "I'll ask if anyone has lost money when we go to the fair tonight."

George frowned, he thought he was helping his family by finding all this treasure. However he could see his Ma was distressed and he didn't want that at all.

"Sorry Ma, I'll try to find out who all this belongs to," George said.

"That would be the right thing to do," Ma said.

"After the fair," George said.

Ma sent him back outside so he could make sure the cows had water before everyone left. His siblings packed up their things and even laid his coat out for him.

George ran to the barn and got the cow's evening meal ready. Feed was put into one trough and water was put into another. The cow bells clacked as the cows all shuffled into the bar ready for an easy meal.

"You all behave while I'm gone." George yelled to the cows as he ran back to the house.

Distant moo's of acknowledgement let him know the cows heard him. It took only five minutes for George to get cleaned up and into his travel clothes, ready for the fair.

His family waited for him at the end of their road and George ran to catch up. Ma and Pa were dividing his siblings between them to keep an eye on as they went to the fair. As he arrived his tall Pa looked him up and down and nodded in approval.

"Ma told me you have a secret friend in the woods today," Pa said with a grin.

"Bandit is quite the well spoken merchant, it takes a lot of skill to trade with him," George replied.

"Well maybe after the fair we can skip your chores and you can help me at the market tomorrow," Pa said with a low chuckle. "Come on George, let's go to the fair."

The short walk to town was filled with excitement as everyone talked around him about what they would win or what food they would try. Paul, his older brother shook his shoulder and looked at him with concern.

"Are you feeling ok, George?" Paul asked.

George put on his biggest smile. "Yeah I'm just thinking a lot. I think I'm going to take a quick walk to clear my head, I'll join you at the games when I get to the fair."

"I'll let Ma and Pa know," Paul said. He then broke out into a grin and elbowed George. "I'll make sure to leave a few prizes for you."

"I think you are mistaken," George said in protest. "I'll leave a few prizes for you."

George and his brother did their secret handshake. Once they patted each other on the back George turned away and went towards the woods. He carefully made sure no one was following him and he dashed towards the old hunter trail.

As the sun started to set and the fair started George saw the shadow up in the clouds. The dragon was going to land and he needed to get to the lake first. He ran as fast as he could, seeing the trees whip by at blinding speed. Thin branches slapped his arms but he ignored the stinging pain and soon he was rewarded.

Ahead of him the trees thinned out and the lake was visible. The large lake in the middle of the woods was usually a calm serene place the villagers came to relax. The calm waters were rippling as if something great had crashed into them, and George stood in awe as something came out of the water.

The great red scaled majestic beast reared its head and sent a wave of water crashing onto the shores. The mighty dragon was as big as the barn, and as it spread its wings it blotted out the setting sun. The large yellow eyes opened and George was face to face with the dragon.

Raising one of his hands, George cleared his throat and did his best to speak clearly.

"Hi."

Chapter 2 - The Quest

The dragon snorted and glared at him. George's smile faded and he started to worry he had made a mistake. The massive creature could probably sneeze and send him flying all the way back to town. Or sit on him and flatten him like a pancake. Perhaps Ma was right and he needed to stop following whatever plan entered his head.

"What do you want, little human?" the dragon grumbled.

The dark gritty voice of the dragon echoed across the lake. The deep tones of the question rumbled the earth beneath his feet and George lost his footing falling to the ground. The dragon took a step onto the beach and brought his head closer.

"Hi Mr. Dragon!" George yelled.

"Bah!" the dragon cried in surprise. He retreated back into the lake and shook his head. "I can hear quite well, please do not scream."

The dragon held a clawed hand on his head just like Ma did when George asked too many questions at once. George feared he might upset the dragon and never get his wish if he bothered him too much.

"I'm sorry Mr. Dragon, I was just really excited to get my wish," George said.

"Wish?" the dragon asked, confused.

The dragon inspected George for several seconds before a look of understanding filled his scaly face. The dragon smiled showing off his fangs, and he lowered his head to look at George directly.

The dragon sighed and spoke in a friendly tone. "Ah the old fable, no one has asked me for a wish in a long time. I would be happy to help-"

"I want to be a dragon!" George said, leaping to his feet. "An orange dragon!"

The dragon lifted his head and laughed. His loud bellow shook the water and sent small waves onto the shore wetting Goerge's feet. After his laughter finally died down the dragon looked at him like Pa did after George did something silly.

"Being a dragon is no easy task. I can see you truly desire it, so I offer you…a quest," The dragon said.

George could hardly believe it. He could be a dragon, he would be able to fly, breathe fire and be strong enough to do all the chores his family could give him. He would be so strong and fast he would have more time to play every single day.

"Yes please Mr. Dragon, I'll do a quest!" George said, bouncing on his heels.

The dragon looked at the saddlebags he wore. They were carefully closed tight, and made of strange leather that all the water rolled off. The dragon took from the bags a giant scroll and giant quill. The man sized feather pen danced in the dragon's hands as he wrote on the scroll for a long time.

George used every ounce of patience he had, he stood respectfully away from the dragon so he could write in peace. When the dragon finally finished writing the scroll shrunk until it was George sized. The pen also shrunk down and the dragon placed them at his feet.

George was a great reader so it only took him a minute to read the entire scroll. It listed that George had wished to become a dragon and that the scroll would turn him into one. There was a catch however, George had to do three tasks.

Each task would earn him new special dragon powers. The first would give him fire, the second would give him wings and finally the third would give him magic. If he accepted the terms then his tasks would appear on the scroll. The final line stated if George did all three tasks his quest was complete, and he could wish to become a boy again.

George held the quill in one hand, poised above the dotted line of the scroll. He looked up to the dragon and asked. "I'll still be a dragon right?"

"Yes, a young one without flight, fire or magic. It takes a lot to be a dragon, and I think it will be a good lesson," the dragon said.

With his question answered George signed the scroll. The quill vanished and reappeared in its giant form in the dragon's claws. Sparkles came off the scroll and surrounded George, slowly raising him into the air. The magic made his hair stand on end and the air smelled like raspberries. A great bolt of energy fired from the scroll and hit him square in the chest.

George hit the ground and he blacked out. The last thing he saw was the dragon rising from the lake and flying far away.

...

George woke with a start and looked around him. The dragon was gone but the scroll remained. He reached towards the scroll to check if it was undamaged but gasped from what he saw. His hand had been replaced by an orange coloured scaly arm ending in sharp claws. His eyes went from the claws and down the length of his arm. It connected to George's new scaly torso.

George rose to his feet and turned his head to look at himself. From his torso all the way down to legs he was now a dragon, minus the wings. His long tail wagged behind him kicking up sand and dirt from the shore. Wanting to save the scroll from the dirt he reached towards it and collapsed onto the ground.

Walking around on four limbs proved to be difficult and it took George several minutes to learn how to take a step without crashing into the ground. He spat out the sand in his mouth and rose to his feet once more.

"Come on, the cows walk around like this, I can do it too!" George said boldly, flexing his new sharp toes.

With slow delicate steps he walked towards the scroll and picked it up. Proud at his accomplishment he cheered and looked around himself for his clothes. Nothing else remained and George looked at the scroll wondering how he was going to carry it home.

His tail whipped behind him and George got an idea. He put the scroll near the end of his tail and watched it in amazement as the tail coiled around it. With the scroll now secure he made his way back home.

As he passed the edge of the lake he paused to check his reflection. A big dragon head with smiling teeth reflected in the lake, he had big yellow eyes and bright orange scales just like he wanted. Finally on the top of his head, he had two big white horns. He looked like the big dragon he always wanted to be.

The sun had vanished completely and the moon had just started to rise, in the reflection just above his head the great white moon looked down. George frowned because it meant the fair was finishing up and now he wouldn't be able to use his new found dragon body to win games. With nothing left to do but go home George set out again excited to show his family.

The path to his home looked smaller than George remembered and he seemed to remember the fence being taller too. The cows watched as he passed by and shook their heads while mooing.

"Go away dragon, this isn't your home!"

George looked around for the speaker but he didn't see anyone. He wasn't familiar with their voices either. He kept his new ears out and used his sharp vision to look for them.

"Down here you scaly oaf!"

George looked down to see a much smaller Ash toss her head up towards him. The cow's calls brought the rest of the cows towards the fence and each of them told him to leave.

"Ash, it's me, George!" George said, laying down on his belly. "I met a dragon and he fulfilled my wish!"

"George, it is you!" Ash gasped. "You're so big now, I can hardly believe it."

"I'm not a real dragon just yet, I have to go on a quest. I just need to talk to Ma first and then I'll check on your food," George said.

He rose and walked towards the house confident that his Ma would be amazed. He could let the horses relax as used the plow all by himself. He could also help Pa carry everything back home from the market. Becoming a dragon had been his best idea.

Ma came out onto the steps looking out at the far field. She was clearly looking for him and not waiting for her to worry he called out.

"Ma, look at me, I'm a dragon now," George said, dancing on the spot.

Ma turned and fell onto the steps. Her eyes were as wide as saucers, and she held her hands to her head as her mouth hung open. George sat down on the ground waiting for his Ma's happy reaction.

"George!" Ma screamed. "What did you do!"

"A dragon granted me a wish Ma. I wished to be a dragon, and it worked," George said.

"George, go fix this right now," Ma said with her hands on her hips. "If you don't you will be grounded."

George was confused, he thought Ma would think this was amazing. He frowned, he didn't want to get grounded. "Ma, if I want to turn back I have to-"

"Then go do it!" Ma said. "I'm going back inside, when I see you again I want regular George, not George the dragon."

"Okay Ma," George said, rising to his feet.

If Ma wanted him to go on the quest that badly then he had too. George remembered the terms of the wish and he checked the scroll. It took a minute for him to get his tail to release the scroll and he had to slap his tail away when it tried to grab the scroll from him.

The scroll had three new lines at the bottom, the spot where his tasks would be for his quest. The final two tasks however were covered in question marks, keeping them hidden from his view. The first was legible thankfully and he read it out loud.

"Find a great treasure," George said. He tapped his finger on his snout as he thought about it. "All dragons have treasures, so that makes sense."

He rolled the scroll back up and gave it to his tail for safe keeping. Rising back to his feet he knew just the person to ask and made his way back to the woods. When he crossed the path of the cows he waved.

"Sorry, Ma said I have to go on the quest now. I'm sure Paul will get your food for you," George said to the cows.

The cows all let out long moos, wishing him good luck and safe travels. Even sassy Ash had tears in her eyes as she lifted a hoof to wave goodbye.

George entered the forest and went to the usual spot he could find Bandit. A hollowed out massive oak tree. It had been struck by lightning years ago and the hollow home was a good size for the big raccoon. As George neared it he heard scratching and a voice.

"That's five more coins to the pile, a broach and even a letter opener. I wonder which I should bring to the kid this time," the voice said from inside the tree.

"Bandit?" George asked.

The raccoon stuck his head out of a hole in the tree at George's eye level. Bandit and him stared at each other for a long time before Bandit opened his mouth to squeak.

"G-G-George?" Bandit stammered, rearing back.

"Hi Bandit! I got turned into a dragon and now I can hear you. Ma said I had to do a quest to return to normal and I need help finding a great treasure," George said.

"Whoa, whoa, whoa there buddy. That's all you had to say, I'm in," Bandit said, rubbing his paws together.

"In?" George asked.

"Yeah, in, I'm coming with you!" Bandit said. "Can't have my good buddy out there getting all the treasure without me."

The raccoon piled all his things into a cloth sack and tied it to a branch. Putting it over his shoulder he hopped down onto George's back. Bandit patted his big belly and looked around.

"Say, do you have any snacks for the road kid?" Bandit asked.

"Oh, I kind of forgot. Ma said I can't come back until I'm a boy again. I guess we could see Mr. Swanson the wood cutter. He's close by and we could trade for some snacks," George said, pointing towards the town.

"Trade?" Bandit gasped. "Well, you are good at getting a good deal. Tell you what, I'll pay if you talk to the guy for me."

With their plan set George walked towards his neighbour's house happy as a well fed cow. His best pal Bandit was with him and together George knew finding a great treasure was the least of his worries.

Chapter 3 - Friendly Faces

Mr. Swanson's cabin was a nice small home at the edge of the woods. The log house looked like it grew right out of the tree line. George had been here many times before to buy firewood, and Mr. Swanson was always nice.

"Mr. Swanson!" George yelled. He stepped over the small fence and sat in front of the door.

"One moment George," the old woodcutter said.

George could hear him get on his boots and the door opened to reveal a sleepy Mr. Swanson. He tugged his sleeping cap off his head and looked at George.

"George, you seem to be a bit taller today," Mr. Swanson said.

"I got turned into a dragon," George said.

The man scratched at his beard and walked around George, inspecting his brand new orange scales. He grumbled in approval of George's new sharp talons and teeth.

"I can see that, is your Ma worried about you?" Mr. Swanson asked.

"She just told me to go on a quest to change back to normal," George said. His stomach growled and George laughed. "I was hoping to buy some snacks."

"Ah, a wise woman indeed. Well if you have some money I can sell you some helpful things," Mr. Swanson said.

He took George and Bandit to his shed. It was packed to the brim with all sorts of supplies and George wondered what he should ask for.

"I can sell you some saddle bags to store them in, and a saddle for your little friend to sit on," Mr.Swanson said, laying them out.

The man laid out the bags, the saddle and lots of wrapped up food. Also on offer were tents and blankets to keep warm at night. George knew a quest could take some time so he would need as much as he could carry. Lucky for him he was now a mighty dragon, so that wouldn't be a problem.

Bandit hopped down and started to look over what was offered. He divided them into a neat pile while the man watched. When he finally decided on what George would need he opened his little pouch.

"Regular folk won't be able to understand me, I need you to talk to him for me George. Tell him I'll give him three gold for all this," Bandit said.

"Bandit says for three gold he will buy everything,"
George said.

"Well tell your friend he has a deal," Mr. Swanson
said.

The man sat on the ground and shook Bandit's little
paw. The gold coins fell into Mr. Swanson's hand and
vanished into his pocket. The two of them then
packed everything on George's back. George took a
step and found it wasn't too heavy for him and now he
was excited to go.

"Good luck in your quest!" Mr. Swanson cried. "Bring
me back a story or two!."

George waved goodbye and merrily skipped down the
road. As he and Bandit made it back into the woods
George had to stop. He felt like he had forgotten
something.

"Bandit, where are we going?" George asked.

"Glad you asked, I have a map," Bandit said.

From his pouch he produced a folded up paper. The
crinkled old paper was stained from juice and crumbs.
When Bandit finally unfurled the paper he showed
George. It was a rough sketch of the area, with a big
X deep in the woods.

"You can read this?" George asked. The map made little sense to him but he believed in Bandit.

"Sure can pal!" Bandit said.

George looked to the sky and noticed how dark it had become. It was night time and he could still see well with his dragon eyes. He could see the frost start to collect on the leaves and a cold wind blew in. George worried it was going to get cold for Bandit and decided to stop.

"Let's set up camp," George said, poking at the saddle bags.

With Bandit's help he set up the big tent and laid out the blankets. Curling up inside it George settled down with Bandit. They opened the food bags and had a snack before falling asleep. George closed his eyes and happily sighed. He was a dragon and he was on a quest.

...

George yawned and woke up Bandit. It was another brand new day and it was time to move. George tried to pack up the tent but couldn't get it back into its bag. Bandit however impressed George as he magically made the tent fit.

"How did you do that Bandit?" George asked. "The only other person I know who can do that is Ma."

Bandit flexed his little paws and smiled. "Raccoon secret, maybe after we get the treasure I can tell you."

George was curious how he did it so he agreed. Bandit stuffed everything back into the saddle bags and crawled onto George's back. They set off again down the road, and George kept an ear out for Bandit's instruction.

"I think you need to take a right at that bush there," Bandit said.

"Bandit, I think we passed this bush before. Are you sure you know where we are going?" George asked.

"One hundred percent. But I just remembered it's supposed to be left when we reach the bush," Bandit said.

George was beginning to think maybe Bandit had the map upside down. He was still having fun with his best pal and merrily walked down the new path.

As the tree's became thicker the road slowly vanished. The road changed from stone blocks into gravel and soon changed to dirt. The unknown forest path was the furthest George had ever been from home. Which meant he must be going the right way.

Ahead in the distance George heard barking. It came through the trees and after the barks he heard a boy yell. George was worried the boy might be hurt and hurried towards the voice.

George found a giant tree in the woods and around the trunk were three wolves. The small wolves hopped around the tree barking up at a white cat tail. There was a big grey wolf, a white wolf and a tiny pup.

"Be careful you might fall!" the largest wolf cried.

"We are friendly!" The white wolf whimpered.

"It's ok, cats are our friends!" the tiny pup said, hoping in place.

George approached the wolves and they all turned to him. He was told to be afraid of the forest wolves but these ones were young and friendly. The wolves sniffed at the air towards him and wagged their tails. George wasn't scared by them at all.

"Hi friendly dragon. We need help to get this cat down a tree," the pup said.

"I'll see what I can do," George said, walking up to the tree. "Hello kitty, please come down. I'm a friendly dragon just like these nice wolves."

There was rustling up near the top of the giant tree. The tail disappeared and two tall white cat ears peaked over the branches. After a few seconds the cat moved into view, but it wasn't a cat at all.

It was a young elf boy with bright white cat ears and a tail. His messy locks matched the fur of his ears and George could see it was full of leaves, twigs and dirt. George had only met an elf once before, he knew they had pointy ears, not cat ears!

"Are you sure they don't want to eat me?" the elf boy asked.

The wolves all howled and danced between George's legs. They promised they were friendly and only wanted to play with the strange looking elf boy. They wanted to chase his tail and play tag.

"They just want to play," George said. He explained to the elf boy what the wolves had said.

"Alright I'm coming down," the elf boy said.

The elf boy tugged on his backpack and started to climb down the tree. He looked scared and went slowly down each branch. When he reached the halfway point his foot slipped and the boy fell.

George rushed to his aid and lifted his head up. The elf boy fell onto the top of his head and held onto his horns. He was shaking, but he was unharmed. George lowered his head down and the elf boy stepped down onto the ground.

The wolves sniffed the elf boy's hand and happily barked dancing around him. The elf boy bowed to George and held out his hand.

"What's your name dragon, and why are you here deep in the woods?" the elf boy asked.

"I'm George, I used to be a human, but now I'm a dragon. My Ma says I have to change back to normal so I'm on a quest," George said, shaking the boy's hand with a claw..

The big wolf howled. "I'm Claw!"

The white wolf cheered. "I'm Cloud!"

The tiny pup squeaked. "I'm Pip!"

Bandit waved from his seat on George's back. "Hi there I'm Bandit."

The elf boy put his hands on his hips as he said. "I'm Eli, nice to meet you all."

George was surprised, it looked like Eli could hear the animals just like him. Maybe he could help him and Bandit find the way through the woods. Perhaps he could even help them find his great treasure.

Pip the tiny wolf snuck up behind Eli and poked his cat tail with his nose. "And you're it!"

George's thoughts were pushed aside as the game of tag started. Eli and the wolves were nimble and small, diving under branches or big roots. George was fast and knew all the tricks about winning at tag, so he always managed to tag someone else. His big dragon body was easy to tag back so he spent most of his time having to run as fast as he could until he got stuck between trees.

The game was over as fast as it started and they all sat together in a circle. There was plenty of food still so he and Bandit shared their snacks. As they ate George shared his story with them.

Claw nodded his head. "It's good you listen to your Ma. We wolves always listen to our mother because she is very wise."

Pip looked up from his snack to agree. "Mother is the best after all!"

Cloud had finished her snack and jumped around excitedly. "I wish we could go on a quest, it sounds fun."

"It is fun. I am very lucky to have my good friend Bandit with me too." George said.

"I'm on my own quest too, a fairy did this to me and I need to find a way to fix it." Eli said, tapping his ears.

George looked at the cat ears on Eli and his curiosity took over. "What happened to you?"

"Well as you know elves always have big fancy names. We get our names and we accomplish something great. I wanted to be the best explorer in my village so I looked for the fairies and made a wish. I wanted to be as graceful as a cat, but look!" Eli said, tugging on his ears.

"They must have gotten mixed up," George said. He tapped on his nose with a claw as he got an idea. "Why don't you come along with Bandit and I, Eli. That way when we reach Mr. Dragon he can help you too."

"That sounds awesome, I'd love to join you on your quest," Eli said, with a huge grin. "I'm an explorer in training so I can help out too."

The wolves wagged their tails but before they could speak their ears all rose. In the distance George heard a wolf call and their new friends leapt to their paws.

"Mother is calling us home for dinner, good luck on your quests!" The wolves shouted their goodbyes as they vanished into the trees in a flash, running towards the distant call.

Eli, George and Bandit waved goodbye watching the wolves vanish from view. Once they were gone Bandit showed Eli where to sit on the saddle. With their new friend secure on George's back they set out again on their journey.

In the corner of his eye he saw Eli turn the map upside down and hand it back to Bandit. Bandit squinted at the map and then slapped his forehead.

"Left at that stump, George," Bandit said.

George smiled and turned down a new dirt road. Having another friend to travel with was twice as exciting, and he couldn't wait to learn his new friend's favourite games. With Eli helping them out they would be on track for this quest in no time.

Chapter 4 - The Yellow Menace

At the start Eli was a bit shy, but as Bandit and George made little jokes the elf boy started to open up. He had all kinds of stories about funny animals like crows tricking smart elves. George felt like this whole quest business was a great idea, he should do more of them after this one.

The map had led them to an open grass field, dotted with tiny houses and farms wrapping around a river. A windmill as tall as George's shoulder spun in slow lazy circles. Yet no one could be seen in the super small village.

"Bandit, are you sure that's a treasure map?" Eli asked.

"What else could it be?" Bandit asked, opening the crinkly page. "Big X and everything, maybe it's hidden in this weird village."

George wasn't sure there would be treasure, unless it was someone's toy models of a village. As George poked his nose against a house that looked like a bakery he smelled fresh bread. Who would make a toy village and make miniature bread?

"George, what are you looking at?" Eli asked.

"I smell fresh bread, it doesn't make any sense. Who would make such a small village, the only person who could fit inside these houses is Bandit," George said.

A tiny voice squeaked from inside the bakery. A tiny woman with a flour covered apron waved at him through the window. George had to lay down on the ground to get close enough to see her.

Her hair was bright green and she had butterfly wings that made her hover above the ground. George couldn't believe it, he had found a village of fairies.

"You must run, there are evil wasps everywhere," she whispered.

Wasps were nasty bugs, they stung and bit George when he and his siblings played outside during summer. Wasps were not very large, but George could see why the tiny fairies were frightened of them. If a wasp was nearly as big as him he would be scared too.

Buzzing could be heard all around them and George looked around for the wasps. Bandit dove into the saddle bags and Eli took out a small sword from his bag. The elf boy's cat ears sprang up moving this way and that looking for the source.

"George… I don't think these are normal wasps," Eli said, pointing to the sky.

Wasps bigger than a fat house cat dropped down onto the tiny village and began eating the crops at the small farms. They dove at the bakery, knocking off pieces of the roof and buzzing angrily at George.

"Hey, stop it!" George yelled. "That isn't yours!"

The wasps in the field looked at George for a second, then turned back to eat the plants. George had to do something, the tiny fairy village was under attack and they were far too small to stop the wasps on their own.

Eli was hiding in a small barn he could barely fit in, holding the sword out while his tail curled around his boots. George had to do something to help his friends too.

A wasp stung George in the nose, the stinger bounced off his hard dragon scales unable to hurt him. The angry, ugly bug in his face still scared him and George took a step back running over the windmill.

"Oops," George said.

The windmill collapsed, falling apart into pieces. The fairies who were hiding inside of it ran away, screaming as they panicked. George looked down at the big wide blades now on the ground and had an idea.

He picked one up in his claws and turned around to meet the angry wasp head on. As the wasp buzzed towards him he swung the windmill blade and splatted the wasp in a single hit.

The fallen wasp gained the attention of the rest of the bugs and soon they started to swarm towards him. Bandit called out from the saddle bags and George could barely hear him over the buzzing.

"George, they are coming from above!" Bandit yelled.

George looked up and saw three of them coming down straight for him. He held onto the windmill blade tightly and swung it like a bug swatter.

Smack!

All three wasps fell from the sky, dropping down onto the ground dead. The evil swarm of bugs became angrier, leaving the crops alone to come attack him.

George ran towards the river, and all the wasps followed. George led them near the water and then started swinging his new bug swatter. Each time he swung he knocked down more and more wasps until the air began to clear. In a few minutes he managed to defeat all the wasps and save the village.

George returned and saw Eli was helping the fairies
move the broken pieces of the windmill. In his haste
to drag the wasps away he had stomped on a barn,
kicked up the fields and broke someone's fence.

George felt terrible, he wanted to save the fairies but
he damaged the village almost as much as the
wasps. George put the bent and now useless windmill
blade onto the broken pile of windmill parts.

"I'm super sorry, I broke your little village when I tried
to defeat the wasps," George said, hanging his head
low.

He was surprised when all the fairies had gathered
around and cheered. They called him brave, and
thanked him for saving them from all the evil bugs.
The little baker fairy walked up to George and did a
happy dance.

"You saved us, great dragon! The evil wasps had
been attacking us for months and now they are all
gone," the baker fairy said.

The other fairies agreed, praising George more. Eli
stood behind them moving from one foot to the other.
He seemed very embarrassed and George wondered
what was wrong.

"I'm sorry George, I was a scaredy cat," Eli said.

George smiled at his new friend. "It's ok, you did the smart thing. The wasps were big and angry, but my scales protected me from their stingers. I'm glad you are safe and that you helped the fairies while I was busy."

"Is there anything we can do to help you?" the baker fairy asked.

"Well I'm George the dragon, and I'm on a quest with my good friends. That's Eli the elf and this is Bandit the raccoon," George said.

Bandit poked his head out of the saddle bags holding onto a sandwich toothpick like a sword. When he saw it was safe he dove out of the bag and stood up holding out his fake sword.

"Bandit and George have done it again, we saved the city!" Bandit yelled.

Eli laughed and patted Bandit's head. "I think it was George who saved the day, Bandit."

Bandit held up a little paw. "It was a team effort, you know."

"What is your quest, great heroes?" The baker fairy asked.

"Right now we are looking for a great treasure,"
George said.

"I love quests like that, it sounds very exciting." the
baker fairy said.

"I need it so I can turn back into a normal boy, have
you seen any treasures?" George asked.

The fairies gathered around and talked to each other.
They brought out tiny cupcakes, thimbles of apple
juice and toys, everything they thought could be a
treasure. They offered the snacks to George but he
didn't feel right taking anything because he damaged
their village so much.

Bandit and Eli snacked on the cupcakes while George
checked his magic scroll. The line for finding a great
treasure was still there, meaning they hadn't found a
great treasure just yet.

"I have a map!" a tiny fairy in a purple hat squeaked.

The fairy ran off before George could say a word.
Bandit was excited to have a new map to look at.
George sighed and was glad Eli was with them so he
could help Bandit read it. He didn't want to get lost
again.

It took four fairies to bring the big map to George and
they unrolled it on the ground. There was a painting of

a great hero wielding a sword and fighting an evil
monster with big claws and fangs. The sword the hero
held shot out bolts of lighting and looked very fancy.

At the bottom of the paper were the directions to go,
showing the path to reach the space where the sword
was hidden. There were haunted woods and traps
dotted along the path. George couldn't believe his
luck, with such a dangerous path the treasure must
be great indeed.

The fairies offered them the map and in exchange
George helped them put the windmill back up. It was
hard work, but with George's mighty strength, and
Eli's sharp eyes helping him they put the windmill
back together. Bandit even helped, passing them
tools or measuring things with a string.

The windmill's blades started to spin again and looked
good as new. That is if you didn't notice the one bent
blade or the chipped paint. As George tilted his head
he could also tell it was slightly uneven now but the
fairies didn't mind. The fairies handed Bandit the map
and everyone hopped back onto George's back.

"Goodbye George the dragon, we hope you and
friends have lots of good luck on your quest!" the
fairies cheered, waving as they left.

"Goodbye forest fairies!" George called back.

George and his friends waved goodbye one last time. They set off down a new road and followed the new map. All of them were excited to find the magic sword, it was the best treasure any of them had heard off.

They followed the road for some time eventually reaching a bridge, stretching across a big river. The bridge was made of big wooden beams and looked to be worn down. Small holes dotted its surface and it didn't look safe at all to George.

"Maybe there's another way around," George said nervously.

"The map says this is the way," Bandit said.

"Maybe you two should go first, I might have to swim across," George said.

Eli hopped down first and walked up to the bridge. He stepped onto the edge of the bridge and they all heard a crack. Wood pieces fell into the river below, vanishing from sight.

"I think we might need to find another way," Eli said, his face pale and he stepped back.

Bandit looked at the map and took out his piece of string. He held it against the map and started to count on his finger. The raccoon hummed and hawed as he counted off numbers.

"Three, carry the four… ah ha!" Bandit cried. "I got it."

Eli and Bandit got back onto George's back and they set off. Bandit told him to go down small dirt trails and pretty soon George wondered if they were lost again.

"Where are we going Bandit?" George asked.

"There is a shortcut, all we have to do is cross the haunted spider infested woods," Bandit said.

George was starting to feel like maybe this quest wasn't as easy as he hoped it would be.

Chapter 5 - Haunted Woods

"We can try to find another way around," Eli said.

He took the map in his hands and looked it over several times. His face was grim and he shook his head. There was only this way, or the dangerous bridge.

"George can squash those evil spiders," Bandit said.

George took a brave step forwards, and then another. Soon he was jogging along the path. Spiders were small, and he was a big dragon. They wouldn't be able to harm him at all.

The trees around them grew bigger and became more densely packed. It grew darker in the woods as the tree tops soaked up the sunlight. The dirt trail they travelled on was a thin winding road, going between the ancient trees.

"This is a very old forest, it must be as old as my great grandpa," Eli said quietly, pulling his hood over his head.

"How old is he?" George asked.

"I think he's about two thousand years old. His birthday is next month so I can ask him again," Eli said.

George was amazed, Eli's great grandpa must know all kinds of wonderful stories. If he was lucky maybe they could visit Eli's home after the quest so he could meet him. He must know lots of new games to teach him too.

"We are nearly there," Bandit said. "Keep going until you reach the stream and follow it to the waterfall. The sword must be hidden nearby."

Bandit rolled up the map and put it back into the saddle bags. He took out a jug of juice and had a drink. After Eli had a sip they gave it to George and he drank the rest of it in one go. Being a dragon was thirsty work.

"I don't think this forest is haunted at all. We haven't even seen any spiders either," George said.

"We might have gotten lucky. Maybe they all moved away since the map was made," Eli said.

Bandit kicked back and layed down, watching the tree tops and yawning. He took out a tiny pillow and blanket, curling up for a nap.

"Wake me up if something exciting happens," Bandit said sleepily.

The next hour was quiet, even the birds and insects kept to themselves not wanting to disturb the raccoon's rest. George did find it odd that a big forest like this didn't have more critters inside it. He started to wonder if they were the only ones here.

Ahead of them was a big fallen tree. The mighty trunk was split open and charred. It must have been hit by a lightning bolt a long time ago causing it to fall down. It crossed the road and left only a small space to get under it.

Eli patted him on the side and motioned for George to crawl under it. George got down onto his belly and slithered like a snake, quickly crossing under the trunk of the once great tree.

As he reached the other side he got back up onto his feet and saw ahead of him a split in the road. He waited for Eli to direct him but he didn't hear or feel anything. As George craned his neck around he didn't see Eli or Bandit.

There was a muffled scream above him and George looked up. High up in the branches he saw Eli and Bandit stuck in silk cocoons. Around them were three scary looking giant spiders. They were almost as big as a horse, and they hissed at George with huge fangs. The sharp black fangs were as long as a sword and looked very deadly.

But George couldn't leave his friends up there, so he
puffed out his chest and challenged the evil spiders.
The monsters crawled down on silk ropes with anger
building in their beady eyes.

George ran up to the tree and kicked off it. As he
swooped into the air he reached out his claws and
slashed the first spider. The monster was quicker than
he expected and dropped down dodging his attack.
The silk rope however was still in reach and George
twisted mid air to cut it.

The spider fell down and crashed into the dirt, dazed
at what happened. George wished he had his wings
to fly up to his friends, but instead he fell to the
ground. As soon as George landed on his feet he bit
at the giant spider, grabbing onto its leg. He spun
around picking the spider up and launched it at
another one.

The spider he threw flipped around end over end and
collided with another spider. They pulled down layers
of webs on top of themselves and got tangled up. The
spiders hissed and spat at George. They had angry
voices he could barely make out.

"Noooo, you have ruined our tasty lunch, go away
dragon!" the spider shouted.

The last spider hovered in the air, choosing instead to
run away, fearful of George's awesome strength.

George stepped towards the two angry stuck spiders and growled at them.

"I'm going to cut you loose but I want you to untie my friends," George said sternly.

The spiders hissed and tumbled around for a minute until they gave up. They sighed, and then agreed to let his friends go. George grabbed onto the webs and cut away the threads, releasing the giant spiders. They climbed back up into the tree and lowered down Bandit and Eli.

George carefully cut them out of the cocoons with his claws and helped them onto his back. George took one more look up into the tree and saw the spiders attempting to rebuild their trap.

"No eating people!" George shouted at them.

The spiders shook their legs furiously at him but agreed. They packed up their webs and walked across the treetops looking for a new hunting spot. Bandit and Eli shook their fists at spiders until they vanished from sight.

"And good riddance!" Bandit yelled at the top of his lungs.

"Thank you George, I was scared we were gonners," Eli said, holding a hand to his chest.

"Thanks a bunch, big guy. You really showed them who's boss," Bandit said.

George felt pretty great, he had saved his friends and possibly more people by sending the spiders away. He flexed his arm to show off to his friends before continuing the journey.

While they all had a good laugh and shared a few jokes George could see everyone was keeping an eye out now. The dense dark upper branches were hidden and could have more monsters lying in wait.

A wailing howl shook the trees around them and they froze. George couldn't take another step as he tried to make sense of the frightening sound. Bandit hid in Eli's backpack pulling the flap closed. Eli trembled, holding his sword at the ready.

The wail rose again and this time they listened. It sounded like words to George but it was too far away to tell. He was scared to get closer and took a step back.

Eli held a hand to his ear and listened very carefully. His cat ears turned towards the source of the sound and the elf boy gasped.

"It's someone asking for help, we need to save them, George," Eli said.

Bandit stuck his nose out of the backpack and wiggled out his head. "What if it's another spider trap?"

There was no way to know for certain, but George wasn't going to let anyone else get eaten by spiders. He waited until he heard the wail again and then ran towards it.

They crashed out of the bushes looking around wildly for who was in trouble. They found in the middle of the road a wagon that had sunk down to its wheels in the mud. The driver was trying to pull it out of the muck by themself as his steed stood beside them.

The driver turned around and this time it was their turn to scream. The driver was a skeleton, with muddy shoes and a big floppy hat on its head. The big feather stuck in the hat bobbed around as the strange person spoke.

"Sorry friends, you found me at an unlucky time. My shop is closed until I get my wagon unstuck," the skeleton said.

"Shop?" George asked, looking at the wagon.

It was a travelling merchant wagon, with spots for the sides to open to show off their wares. It was always an exciting time when merchants with similar carts showed up to his village with fun treats and tales of far away places.

"My name is Chris, owner of the Wonder Wagon Shop. This is my faithful horse Sally," Chris said.

George could see through the horse and saw it glowed a light blue. George realized that Sally was a ghost horse.

As Sally heard her name she tossed her mane and pawed at the ground. She picked up the wagon's straps and gave it a pull, but the wagon didn't even move.

Eli was as confused as George was, he raised a finger and asked the merchant. "Why are you a skeleton, and why do you have a ghost horse?"

"I made a wish with a dragon of course!" Chris said, delighted at the question. "As a human with a short life I didn't know if I would be able to see the entire world so I asked to be able to live forever. Next thing you know, I'm a skeleton and now I can travel the world for as long as I want.

Bandit hopped off George's back and looked up to Chris. He held out a paw to the man and shook his skeletal hand.

"As a fellow trader I offer you my help, we can get you unstuck in no time. My friend George is the strongest guy I know," Bandit said.

"I would be grateful for the help, it is a blessing you came to our rescue," Chris said.

The skeleton man and his horse stepped out of the way letting George try to free the wagon. He gripped the wagon's straps and tried to drag it out of the mud. The wagon's wheels turned and it started to rise up, but George felt his feet slide on the dirt and the wagon slid back into the mud.

George looked down to his dragon hands and tried again. He was a mighty dragon, how could mud stop him?

George heaved and pulled but no matter what he tried the wagon was just stuck. It sank even lower in the mud and Chris threw up his arms.

"My life's work, it cannot be! How cruel is fate to do this to an honest merchant," Chris said, sitting down on a log.

"Chris, you might have found something to save your wagon," Eli said. He pointed to the log under Chris. "We can use it as a lever to help lift the wagon for George."

"That's a great idea, let's give it a try," Chris said.

Chris, Bandit, Eli and Sally rolled the log under the wagon. Eli asked George to put a rock under it and they lifted the log up while George put the rock in place. Now the big log looked like a giant seesaw.

Eli jumped up on the end log and waved over everyone. "We need to push down on this while George pulls out the wagon."

With everyone in place George took the straps up again. His friends jumped on the seesaw and pushed the wagon up into the air and out of the mud. As soon as it was free of the mud George pulled with all his strength and saved the wagon. Its wheels touched solid ground again and it rolled up to George bumping him on the nose.

"You did it!" Chris said, clapping his hands. "Please let me reward you."

"It's ok sir, we are already looking for treasure. We are finding a magic sword hidden around here," George said.

"Oh you're on a quest. In that case I insist, let me give you some food for your travels. If you are talking about the magic fairy sword, I heard it's hidden behind a waterfall," Chris said.

The travelling merchant opened his wagon and they saw fantastical wares from all over the world. Swords and spices, paintings and jewels. Bandit tapped his fingers together as he stood in awe of all the fancy items.

Chris put into George's saddle bags a few more days worth of food and water. He thanked them again for freeing him from the mud and got into his seat.

"If you are looking for places to go, my town of Sleepy Hollow is that way," George said.

After pointing Chris in the right direction the merchant took off, his ghost horse Sally taking the wagon out of sight.

They looked at the map and realized they were close. They ran the rest of the way, reaching a waterfall by a lake.

George had them take off the saddle bags so he wouldn't get their blankets wet. He then dove into the water and paddled along to the waterfall. The water beat down on his back and George had to power through the strong current to get behind it. When he managed to make it he saw a small cave, and inside it was a glowing chest.

He took it in his jaws and swam back to shore bringing it to his friends. They gathered around the big glowing chest and held their breath as George opened the lid.

Inside was a beautifully made silver sword. It had a lightning bolt etched down the sharp blade and the gemstone in the sword's hilt shone brightly with electric blue light. George took it out of the chest and held up, catching the sunrays.

"Try to use the lighting powers," Bandit said, poking at George's side.

The sword was too small for him to hold and felt more like a butter knife rather than a hero's sword. George pointed it at a nearby rock and looked down at the sword. He wasn't sure how to make it shoot lighting, but it couldn't be too hard.

"Lightning bolt!" George shouted.

The gemstone flashed and the end of the sword zapped the rock with a big blue bolt. The rock exploded sending little pieces into the air and they all cheered.

"What are you going to do with it George?" Eli asked.

George wasn't sure. It was too small to fit his dragon hands and he was already really strong. After he thought about it for a second he handed the sword to Eli.

"Are you sure George?" Eli asked. "It's the treasure you need for your quest."

"My task was to find a great treasure, and I did it. I think having good friends is a much better treasure than just an old sword. I would rather you have it in case I'm the one needing saving next," George said.

The saddlebags started to hover in the air and the special scroll popped out. It opened itself up and a golden check mark appeared next to his first task. A new task started to appear and they all gathered around. When the scroll finished writing his next task he looked at his friends.

"This will be a fun one. It's a good thing you have me around," Bandit said.

Eli held the sword tightly and nodded his head. "You have my help too."

George felt deep in his chest something changed with him. His breath came out hot and he saw little sparks. The first task was finished and now he could breathe fire. With his friend's help and his new dragon power they would be ready for this next task.

To earn his wings he would have to defeat a mighty foe.

Chapter 6 - Bridge Toll

The good thing was Bandit kept to his word, and George learned a new skill from Bandit. George could repack the saddlebags all by himself and it would stay tidy, Ma would be proud.

The bad thing was they were hopelessly lost. With no real direction George had just walked until they reached a road. They had made it out of the haunted spider forest and were met with a wonderful sight. A road, crossing the plains with the sun high in the air warming them up.

"Which way?" George asked, looking both ways.

The road stretched towards the horizon in either direction, a straight narrow bit of stone cutting the otherwise grassy fields in half. It felt strange and almost wrong how the perfect balance of nature had the grey road split it apart.

"When in doubt, go right, I say," Bandit said, raising his paws. "The one that's an L is left, so this way!"

With nothing else to go on but gut feeling George went right. His big dragon legs made them cross the countryside quickly but he still didn't see any changes. Just fields, sun, the road and the forest.

The road rose to crest a hill and when George reached the top he gasped. His friends leaned out of the saddle and Bandit screamed as he fell to the ground unharmed. Ahead of them was the great and mighty Lake Spockell, with its golden sand coast and crystal clear water.

George ran towards the lake, kicking up dirt behind him. Everyone was happy, and talked about dipping their feet into the water. The hot sun overhead was beating back the fall chill which meant it would be a perfect day to relax.

George ran faster than a horse, and when he reached the sandy beach he kicked up a wave of sand. His friend spat and threw up their arms as they got coated in the fine gritty powder. George slowed down but the damage was already done, his friends were covered in sand and his bag was now full of it.

"Oops, sorry," George said.

Eli smacked the side of his head and tilted it, sand pouring out of his cat ears. The elf boy frowned and grumbled like an old man. He shook his tail and more sand spewed out everywhere.

Bandit was buried in the sand with only his snout out of the pile and he weakly croaked a single word. "Help."

George picked up Bandit by the scruff of his neck and shook the little raccoon, freeing him of the block of wet sand. Bandit's eyes blinked as the poor little guy was dizzy and George set him down.

"Who are they?" Eli asked, pointing towards the shore.

George followed his finger and saw on the beach a little shack next to a dock. On top of the dock sat two men, one was fishing while the other had a blank canvas in front of him.

They walked over the beach and stepped onto the dock approaching the men. As they got closer the fisherman reeling in a trout and gave it to the painter. The painter then dipped the fish in a bucket of paint and used it as a brush. Once the man put down a few lines he washed the fish off and put it back into the lake.

"What are you doing mister?" George asked.

The two men turned around with smiling faces. George and his friends were in awe of their long snowy beards. They had braided them, putting little sea shells or silver coins at the ends of them so when the wind blew it sounded like wind chimes.

"Oh, us old wizards are just enjoying a sunny day on the beach. Winter is coming and we need to head south soon. My name is Tom and this fisherman is my friend Mike," the old painter said.

"Howdy," Mike said, rolling a pipe around in his mouth.

"Hi, I'm George and these are my friends. We are on a quest," George said, striking a pose. The sun reflected off his dragon scales and coloured the dock in orange light.

"A quest you say? We used to give those out back in the day. Chosen one this and ancient secret city that. Glad to see you youngsters are still going out to make a name for yourselves," Tom said.

Mike caught a big fish with spikes on its sides and reeled it in. When Tom used it to paint the canvas it tore up the painting and flicked paint everywhere. Tom then washed it and put it back in the lake watching it go.

"Perfect, a masterpiece. Thank you Mike," Tom said, lifting his painting up and tossing it into the water.

Tom waved his hands and the waves rose up to pick up the painting in a watery fist. The fist threw it high into the air towards the middle of the lake. Mike removed the pipe out of his mouth and spat out a fireball exploding the painting in the air. A trail of ash fell down, the only thing left to show there had been a painting.

"Yup, another good one Tom," Mike said. He waved his fishing pole and turned it into a wand.

"My name is Eli, and I was wondering if you could help us. We are looking for a great foe to defeat so George can get his dragon wings," Eli said, bowing to the wizards.

"A great foe…haven't seen one in ages around these parts. Well, except for a really dangerous one," Tom said, tugging on his beard.

The sound of wind chimes had stopped and under the wizard's great white beard was Bandit untying the coins and sea shells stuffing them into his pouch. The wizard didn't notice, not even Mike did when Bandit started to untie his beard too.

"What foe would that be, great wizards?" Eli asked. His cat ears flat on his head as he tried to keep his eyes off Bandit.

The coins on Mike's beard vanished too and Bandit tried to tip toe away with his ill gotten gains. Mike leaned down and scratched Bandit behind the ears and the raccoon froze, instead offering the coins and sea shells to him.

"Thank you little friend, wind must have knocked them off." Mike took the stolen goods back and tucked them into a pocket.

"A witch," Tom said, with a smile and a bit of glee. "No one has ever defeated her. She is sharp as a needle and strong as an ox. Follow the bridge, take a right through the forest and you can find the witch's house!"

"Good luck," Mike said.

The two wizards waved and vanished in a giant puff of smoke. They took with them the painting supplies and the shack. As soon as the wizards were gone George and Eli looked at Bandit.

"Was just helping them, I'm a raccoon so I see these things you know," Bandit explained.

Bandit didn't convince either of them, but no harm was done and now they had a foe to face. But first was time for the beach.

They took an hour to take a quick swim and stretch out on the beach, letting the warm sun dry them off. George felt fantastic as the sun warmed up his scales as he laid out like a cat. He was just about to snooze when his friends woke him up for lunch.

They had to dig out the food from the bags since they were still full of sand. Bandit offered to clean out the saddle bags as an apology and the boys accepted. Soon they had a nice easy meal, clear of sand.

They loaded everything back up and George started to circle the lake looking for the bridge. Eli with his sharp eyes pointed at the distance and George focused his eyes seeing the bridge cross the vast lake.

They approached the end of the bridge closest to them and saw a little wooden toll booth with its arm blocking their way. A little bell was on the edge of the booth and George tapped it with a claw.

The door to the booth opened and a big troll got out. He had a tiny top hat on his head and a vest that was three sizes too small. The Troll took off the top hat and gave them a great big bow.

"Welcome to the toll troll bridge toll. For the low, low price of three gold coins you can cross my wonderful bridge. If you are short on funds you can answer a riddle instead," the troll said.

George didn't like the idea of paying so much, three gold was a fortune. He could buy another saddle with all the kit for that kind of money, or a fancy new suit for Pa. They really needed to get across the bridge or it would take all day to get to the witch's house. Which meant it was time for a tricky riddle.

"We would like to try the riddle please," George said.

"What weighs more, one hundred pounds of feathers or one hundred pounds of steel?" The troll asked.

"They weigh the same," Eli said.

"Wrong!" The troll yelled, raising his hands into the air.

A giant bag of feathers rose into the air and ripped apart, dropping soft white feathers all around the troll. Eli yelled and tugged on George's ear. Unsure what was happening George jumped to the side just in time to dodge a huge blacksmith's anvil falling where he just was.

"That's not very nice, someone could get hurt," George said, puffing up his chest. "You can't do that Mr. Troll."

The troll started laughing and sneezed as the feathers kept falling on him. He sneezed so hard he blew feathers up into the air and spat everywhere. He then slapped his big belly and grinned. "Well you lose the riddle so you can't cross."

"George we got to chase off this guy, he's taking people's money leaving them broke or hurting them with his riddle," Bandit said, balling up his fists. "We can take him."

Eli lifted his new sword and said to his friends. "I'll hit him with a bolt, Bandit you try to trip him and George you can breathe fire. Trolls are scared of fire."

With everyone agreeing with the plan they spread out and walked up to challenge the troll. He was taller than George with big arms and a scary toothy smile, but he was alone, George had his friends.

"We are here to banish you troll, your reign of terror is over!" Eli cried, raising the sword.

"Ha, if you think you can chase me with a little sword, you're wrong cat boy," the troll said.

Eli pointed the sword at him and yelled. "Lightning bolt!"

The bolt hit the troll in his vest and made him stumble. Bandit ran behind him and threw down a bag of marbles making the troll wildly dance as he tried to keep his balance.

George huffed but only a spark came out of his mouth. He tried again, huffing as hard as he could but only managed to make a bit of smoke rise out of his nose.

"What dragon has no fire?" asked the troll.

The troll had managed to get his balance and he
pushed George, sending him into the booth. The little
toll booth shattered apart and the wood pieces flew
into the air. The troll then chased Bandit and Eli trying
to catch them in his clawed hands.

George had to save them, but the troll was stronger
than him. He couldn't fight the troll head on, he
needed his fire breath. He got back up and his foot
sank in the piles of feathers, which gave George an
idea.

"Hey Mr.Troll!" George shouted, getting his attention.

When the troll turned to him and his friends got out of
the way, George raised a feather and tickled his nose.
His nose twitched and before George could stop
himself a wave of fire erupted out of his mouth.

The troll ran as fast as he could, out pacing the
flames. George chased him, sneezing again and
breathing out more fire. Tears filled George's eyes
and he had to stop before he ran into a tree. When he
could see again there was no troll in sight, they had
chased him off.

He met back up with his friends, glad to see they were
safe. They removed the scraps of wood, the feathers
and the anvil making sure it was safe for people to
cross.

Bandit came out with a can and gave it to Eli. Eli looked into the can and gasped, running over to show George. Inside the can was over a hundred gold coins, the money the troll had collected.

"We can use it to help people get food," George said.

"We can get medicine for them too," Eli said.

"We could keep it," Bandit said. When George and Eli frowned at him, he held up his paws. "I'm kidding, this troll was a highwayman, stealing from good folk. We should use it to help people."

With everyone ready to go they crossed the bridge, ready to face the witch. What the others didn't know was George put a few feathers into the bags, just in case.

Chapter 7 - A Foe of Might and Magic

The bridge spanned the entire lake, a feat of great building from the greatest minds of the empire. The road surface was perfectly flat, and the sides had plenty of space to look down at the lovely lake water, with schools of fish rising out of the waves.

"I'm surprised the troll didn't count as a mighty foe," Eli said. "He was so big and strong, he could have flattened Bandit and I like a pancake."

"That was a close one, good thing our buddy George is always here to save the day," Bandit said, patting George on the side.

"As soon as I started to breathe fire he ran away, so he wasn't very brave," George said.

The bridge journey was quiet and it let George soak in the sights. The sun was still out beating back the coming fall frost and the lake breeze was fresh. George took in a deep breath of air feeling it all the way down to his toes.

The end of the bridge came into sight and beside it was a big sign. The sign was telling people about the toll on the other side of the bridge. As George reached it he kicked the sign down, no more trolls trying to get tolls.

The road split into four ways, with ways to get to the wizard's academy, the capital, and the great circus. The final road led directly into the forest and it vanished from sight under the great trees there. Dark bark trunks and green needles made up the foreboding wall of nature.

"Let's go George, if we move quickly we can defeat the witch before the sun sets," Eli said.

"There's no haunted forest or giant spiders this time around," Bandit said.

Bandit was right, there was just the witch in there which meant he only had to worry about one danger. George set off with his friends confident they would be able to take on anything the woods threw at them.

After an hour he found out the woods was a really relaxing place just like the lake. Crows and other birds sang above them in trees, their fun light hearted songs filling him with glee. The crows had some funny songs and sounded like pirates while the song birds had more gentle tales. The best part of being a dragon was getting to talk to so many new animals.

"Let's stop for a break in there," Eli said, calling George's attention to a clearing.

The sunny spot of grass between the trees was full of brightly coloured purple flowers. There were berries on bushes and a spot for a campfire. Someone had previously rolled a few logs in place for seats and it looked like a picture perfect camp spot.

"It's getting pretty late, why don't we take on the witch tomorrow?" George asked his friends.

They all agreed and they set up camp, enjoying their food next to a warm fire as the sun set. The full moon rose over the forest and it painted their campsite in liquid silver. It was so bright George was worried he might not be able to get to sleep tonight.

Bandit and Eli were already fast asleep in their blankets, snoring peacefully. George was feeling exhausted too after the exciting day and curled up to sleep, wrapping his tail around himself. His eyes felt heavy and soon he was snoring next to the flowers.

"George, wake up!" Bandit yelled, slapping George in the face with his little paws.

"Five more minutes please," George groaned.

"George, I think we have a problem here," Eli said. His voice was muffled and sounded far away.

George cracked open an eye and found he was surrounded by vines and purple flowers. The odd plants from the day before had completely taken over the clearing and Eli was buried under the plants. Only Bandit was able to wiggle free it seemed.

George tried to rise, but felt the vines squeeze around him trying to hold him down. No silly plants could stop a dragon however, and George flexed his muscles breaking the plants apart. He used his sharp claws to tear apart the plants and freed Eli. He put his friends on his back and left the clearing going back to the road.

"That was very odd. Are you two ok?" George asked.

"I'm fine I think," Eli said, checking himself for cuts.

"Just covered in this purple powder." Bandit said, shaking his fur and sending a plume of purple dust into the air.

George was covered in it too and Eli had so much on him his cat ears and tail were purple now. The elf boy scratched at his ears sending the powder everywhere and turned his ears back to white.

"I don't feel any different, so I think we are fine," George said.

His friends both felt normal so with nothing left to do they continued their journey to the witch's house. The road twisted between the trees until it reached a river, and beside the fast flowing river was a quaint little house.

"The house of our foe, the witch," Eli said, holding a hand over his eyes. "I don't think anyone is home."

George got closer to the house, if his foe wasn't home he would have to wait for them to get home. The house had a small fence around it to protect the nice little garden inside. There were all kinds of edible plants he could see, carrots, potatoes and cucumbers. But there was also a bright red orb hanging from a vine.

"Ick, tomatoes," George said, sticking out his tongue.

"I like tomatoes," Eli said.

"Well then you can have any I get then," George said.

"Get away from my garden you thieving dragon!" a woman yelled behind them.

George turned around ready to fight the terrible and evil witch. But instead of an old scary lady with black robes and a pointed hat he saw something else. A tall mighty woman with a glowing walking stick. Her skin was green and she had fangs meaning George had met an orc. She looked him up and down in turn and raised an eyebrow at him.

The woman swung the stick and it cracked off his forehead making George see stars. As she lifted it to bonk him on the head again, George tried to breathe fire, only for a puff of smoke to tickle the witch's face.

Bonk!

George shook his head and stepped back, breaking the fence behind him. The orc witch grew furious and George, lacking his fire, turned around to run. She shook the stick and chased him. She kept swinging it at George and his friends, no matter how fast they ran..

"Hold still, dragon or else!" she yelled, swinging the staff wildly.

"George, just breathe fire at her!" Eli cried, holding on for dear life.

"Come on big guy, we can take her," Bandit said. "Take this!"

Bandit threw a pine cone but the witch batted it back straight at him striking him in the forehead. Bandit held onto face and hid behind Eli instead.

"Nevermind, keep running," Bandit said.

George ran around the fence with the witch hot on his heels. Each time he slowed down he got a smack on his side from her glowing weapon. The purple powder on his scales vanished with each strike from her and he was wondering if it was protecting him from her spells.

The witch jumped ahead cutting off his route and George had to turn on the spot, ending up against the bank of the fast flowing river. He was backed into a corner with him and his friends in danger. He took out a feather and readied himself to take on the witch.

"Dragon, hold still, you don't know what you're doing," the witch said.

George held the feather in front of his nose and tickled it. His nose twitched and his face scrunched up as the fire deep inside him stirred. He shuddered as he tried to hold in the sneeze. When he failed he opened his mouth and let it out.

"Achoo!" George thundered.

From his mouth the force of the sneeze let out a wave of bubbles, not fire. The bubbles rose up into the air and popped a few seconds later. Everyone was just as confused as him. Except for the witch that is.

"I told you, hold still!" the witch said, shaking her walking stick.

The stick tapped him on the head and sides as the witch walked around him hitting him everywhere the purple powder was on his scales. Eli and Bandit hid away from the witch but they didn't escape from her glare.

"Come here, before the poisonous trickster affects you too," the witch said, jumping over George's back.

"We're fine, we are just meow!" Eli said. He tried to speak again but every word came out the same. "Meow, meow. Meow!"

"Hit me, hit me before something weird happens!" Bandit cried, shaking his hands trying to get the witches' attention.

Bonk! Bonk!

The purple powder vanished from both of them and Eli's voice returned to normal.

"What was that stuff?" Eli asked.

"Poison trick, a nasty purple flower that only grows under the moon. It was made by an evil witch a long time ago, and I've been trying to get rid of it." the witch said, crossing her arms over her chest. "Now why are you here ripping up my yard?"

"The wizards said there was a mighty witch here and I need to defeat a powerful foe for a quest," George said. "It's the only way to get my wings."

"Two wizards? Tom and Mike?" the witch asked.

"Yes, those two great and mighty wizards sent us." Bandit said. "We didn't know you were nice!"

The witch tapped her foot and looked over George. "I was wondering where your wings were. But I have never been defeated, not in riddles, not in arm wrestling, not even in checkers."

George loved checkers, he was the best checkers player in the whole village. He also rather not fight the witch, not just because she was so strong, but also for saving him and his friends from an evil magic plant.

"How are we going to defeat her then George?" Bandit asked.

"Riddles didn't go well last time we tried," Eli said.

"I wish to challenge you to checkers," George said to the witch. "If I defeat you then I'm sure to win my wings for sure."

The witch smiled and held out a hand towards him. "Names Marla, what's yours dragon?"

"George, George the dragon," George said, shaking her hand.

Marla went into her home and returned with a board and a box full of pieces. She set it up in front of her deck and pulled up a chair for herself. She let George pick his colour and he chose black so he could take the first move.

"I am warning you George, you will find me your toughest opponent yet," Marla said, grinning to show off her fangs.

"Then it will make getting my wings all the sweeter," George said, sliding his first piece forwards. "Your turn."

The match went quickly. George would slide his pieces forwards and Marla would match him. Soon he started to jump her pieces and captured three before she even took a single piece of his. As he moved one piece into place and removed his claw he realized his mistake too late.

"Ah, thank you," Marla said.

She jumped four of his pieces matching him for pieces on the board now. She had set him up and

76

George had fallen for her trap. Soon she started making moves all over the board, fighting him back and turning the game around.

George was starting to sweat and Bandit offered him a blanket. George wiped his brow and kept playing, trying his hardest to turn the game around. Marla was aggressive and moved to claim a double piece. George looked around carefully to see what could be done.

Marla had over-extended in one area and if he could get her to take the bait he might be able to move in to turn the game around. He moved a piece forward, an easy capture for Marla and the witch smiled, falling for the trap.

"Thank you, Marla," George said, leaping a single piece across the board. "King me."

The witch started to play more carefully but George had already turned the game back in his favour. With his new king piece causing havoc he was unstoppable. Soon there were only three pieces for Marla and five for George.

The game moved slower, each player carefully moving their pieces. The sun had reached high noon and it beat down on them as they reached the final showdown. Four pieces for George and one for Marla.

He chased her into a corner but a misstep caused a loss of one of his pieces leaving him with three.

He inched forwards, trapping her into a corner. With no moves remaining Marla sighed, moving her piece and George took it finishing the game with only black remaining, the red all captured.

"Good game," George said, holding out his hand.

"Good game, I'm honoured to say I lost to a dragon," Marla said.

"Sorry I thought you were an evil witch at first, I guess I should ask before I assume someone is bad," George said.

"Oh don't worry, I'll have a talk with Tom and Mike about sending people my way without telling them first," Marla laughed.

The scroll rose out of his bags and glowed gold as it unfurled. With the task of defeating a powerful foe completed a new one started to appear. George, his friends and the witch gathered around as they watched the writing appear. When it was done they all gasped.

How was George going to complete this one?

Chapter 8 - Gifts

"Stand on the moon?" Bandit asked, checking the scroll again. "How are you going to do that George?"

George scratched at his head and yelped in surprise as his new wings flashed into the world on his sides. George looked at them and then the sky. The clouds overhead already seemed far out of reach, and the moon would be even further than that. He sighed and flopped onto the ground in defeat with his new wings drooping.

"I'll be stuck as a dragon forever," George said. He covered his snout with his claws and huffed. "My mom is going to kill me."

Marla the witch took the scroll and looked over it a few times. She hummed to herself as she sat down and seemed to be deep in thought. She stood so still George wondered if she had turned into a statue.

"I got it!" Marla shouted, rising to her feet. "It must be a riddle, and I just happen to know that there is an old lunar temple somewhere near. Go to the church down the road and tell the priest I sent you."

Marla handed the scroll back to George and gave directions to the nearby church. George was sad to leave the nice witch so soon but knew he needed to complete his quest first. As they left they all said their goodbyes to Marla and travelled at a brisk pace.

The forest road was less frightening than when they first entered the witch's woods. The sun broke out of the forest canopy and warmed up George's scales. Eli and Bandit stretched out on his back, enjoying the warmth coming off the dragon scales. While his two friends lazily rested George hiked along the road, trying to keep his back steady so they didn't fall off.

The broken uneven road started to smooth out under his talons and soon enough became an even well made road again at the edge of the woods. With the tree line behind him George could see a sunny valley nestled between two mountains, with a lovely little village like his home next to a river. Just outside the village was a big stone church with a tall tower. Inside the tower George saw a shiny bronze bell that caught the sunlight and shone like a beacon.

"That's the church right there. You move as fast as a horse George," Eli said in amazement.

"At this rate we could cover half the world by lunch tomorrow," Bandit said.

"I'm not that quick, Bandit," George said with a light hearted laugh.

They weren't getting closer to standing on the moon by chatting so George lightly jogged towards the church. Coming out of the village was a caravan of merchants who waved to them as they passed by. The merchant men tossed trinkets or coins to his friends on his back claiming that crossing paths with a dragon was good luck.

While the merchants were happy to see them, their steeds were not. The horses tossed their manes and pulled away from George. The horses mumbled to each other around their reins and George had to listen hard to hear them.

"These mad men might sell us to the beast for a snack if we aren't careful, Becky," one chestnut mare said.

"Then I wouldn't have to deal with the merchant's daughter putting bows in my mane every week," a grey mare shot back.

George smiled at the horses and thanked the men for their gifts. He scratched at his chin what to give them back in return and watched a few loose scales fall to the grass. He picked them up and offered them to the merchants who happily took them. They put little holes in the scales and put them on strings to wear as good luck charms.

"I have an idea," Bandit said, rubbing his paws together. "We can take a little detour to town and make a fortune selling dragon scale charms to people. By the time we leave we can be kings!"

George and Eli looked at each other. They rolled their eyes at Bandit's scheme and wished the merchants well on their journey. Eli hopped off his back and together they marched the rest of the way to the church hoping the priest had the answers they needed.

The stone church was a tall building, taller than any other back in his home village. Even with his great height as a dragon the building was still intimidating. The stained glass windows had images of heroes, gods and magical beasts in great detail. There were even flying dragons on a few of them, and one even looked like George with his orange scales.

The giant doors to the church burst open and an overweight priest charged out at them with a staff in hand. He brandished the gold capped pole in their direction as if to challenge them to fight.

"Back beast, I shall not allow you to take the relics from his holy place!" he cried.

"Hi mister, Marla the witch said you could help me on my quest," George said.

The priest blinked in confusion for a few seconds. He lowered the weapon and cleared his throat, looking rather embarrassed.

"I'm sorry, great dragon. Please feel free to sit and I can offer what wisdom I have." the priest said. He bowed and added. "Brother Marvin, at your service."

"I'm George. This is my friend Eli the elf, he has a little bit of a cat issue at the moment. Then this is my pal, Bandit the raccoon," George said, showing off his friends.

"George you say?" Brother Marvin asked with a bit of amusement. He tugged at his greying beard in thought. "Last time I heard about George and a dragon it was quite a different tale."

Bandit hopped forwards and took out the can of gold coins from the bridge toll troll. The heavy can nearly tipped him over and Brother Marvin crouched low to see what the raccoon was offering him.

"An evil troll was taking people's money at the lake bridge. I think it would be best if we gave it to you so you could help the villagers and people passing by," Bandit said.

Brother Marvin looked into the can and was shocked at the vast wealth. Eli translated for the priest, letting him know what Bandit had said. Brother Marvin was delighted, and pet Bandit between his ears.

"I will see that it's put to good use, the poor shall be fed and the sick shall be healed. May the sun father bless you all on your journey," Brother Marvin said, putting a hand on each of their foreheads to bless them.

Bandit tapped on George's wrist for his attention and the little raccoon whispered to him. "Think this guy has spare supplies we could buy?"

George cleared his throat and showed the priest the scroll. After explaining his situation the wise priest nodded and hummed to himself. Once he had been caught up George asked him if he had any gear or advice he could give them.

"There's some old gear kicking around that would be perfect for you and I would be happy to share it with some young men on a quest. If you would be willing to help me, you can have it," Brother Marvin said.

"Sure thing, Brother Marvin. What can we help with?" Eli asked.

It turns out it was an easy side quest that would barely take up any time. All they had to do was wait for dinner time and ring the shiny church bell. Unfortunately the ladder to reach the top was under repairs which meant someone had to climb a tall tower by themselves to reach it.

The inside of the church was huge. It was awe inspiring and George was able to stand at his full height and still had room to jump. The ceiling was covered in colourful art depicting more heroes and gods of worship. The holy grounds brought a sense of peace to their hearts, except for the massive climb they would have to do.

"I think I might have thrown my back out with that troll fight…" Bandit said, he then started coughing into his fist. "Might have a little bit of the old plague too, no climbing for this raccoon.

"George is too heavy to climb these walls. His claws would damage the stone carvings and art too so we can't risk it," Eli said. The elf boy gulped and went pale as his tail tucked between his legs. "I know I wanted to be the best explorer ever, but I could settle by trying to be the best climber ever."

To reach the bell Eli would have to free climb up the tower without any support. It was a dangerous climb and George felt fear grip his heart. If he was still a boy it would take him forever to reach that high and he might get tired before reaching the top. His friend however needed help and they needed the equipment the priest offered too.

"I'll be right here to catch you if you fall, Eli. You have the hero's sword which means not only are you the best climber but also the bravest. If you don't want to try to do this we can ask the priest if we can try something else. This does look like a risky climb," George said.

The little speech gave Eli some courage and they thought together if it was even worth it to try. As Bandit and George discussed other things they could offer to do as chores for the priest he noticed an absence of their other friend. When George looked around all he caught was a flash of white as Eli was halfway up the wall.

"Eli!" George shouted in a panic. "You should have told us you were climbing!"

Eli paused and looked down from his high vantage point. He took a second to catch his breath and once he was secure and sitting on a thin beam up in the air he waved down to George and bandit.

"Then I would have second guessed myself. It's a minute to dinner time and I'm not going to fail Brother Marvin," Eli said, sounding confident.

He hopped onto the wall and kept climbing up the stone walls of the tower, reaching out to find small hand holds between the tightly fitted stones. George and Bandit could only sit with baited breath as their friend climbed higher and higher until he reached the top platform and disappeared from view.

The seconds ticked by and the pulling of a rope could be heard. A deep ring shook the church's walls as the shiny bell clanged loudly above them. It was so loud George wondered if he would go deaf and if Marla could hear them all the way back in her little forest home.

Once Eli had rung the bell three times like they had been asked he appeared at the edge of the platform and started his long climb back down. He was careful and only moved a few feet at a time. George stood under him, ready to spring into action.

Eli was just out of reach as he slipped while trying to grab onto a rocky outcrop. There was a moment of panic as the young elf was freely hanging over a long drop to the floor below. His ears were flat against his head and his tail's fur was sticking on its end. He swung his hand up and managed to catch onto the wall, pulling himself back into a safer spot.

They all breathed a collective sigh of relief and once Eli had a brief moment to recover he finished his climb down to the ground. Bandit ran up and hugged his legs. Eli sat down on the ground and gave the raccoon a hug back.

"That was…a little scary," Eli said, fighting to keep his voice steady.

"You really are an awesome climber!" George said in amazement. He then got an idea and scratched at his chin. "How do elves usually get their titles Eli?"

"When they do something great, an elder or great magical being who recognizes their accomplishments can gift them a new name or a title," Eli explained.

Well George was lacking a little in the magic department at the moment and he was still really young, but he felt like it should still count. George rose to his feet first and stood in front as Eli, holding out his wings and trying to appear magical. Eli and Bandit jumped up onto their feet and wondered what their friend was up to.

"I, George the dragon, recognize the brave actions of Eli the elf. The chosen wielder of the hero's lightning sword. You have helped chase the evil troll from the bridge spanning the Lake Spockell, and have climbed the tower of terror. I name you, Eli the hero!" George said, raising his voice and shouting his friend's name with as much might as he could.

Eli looked embarrassed as Bandit cheered for him. He politely coughed into his hand and said. "I'm not sure that counts, George. I appreciate it however."

Brother Marvin walked into the church carrying a heavy bag and a stack of clothes. He set it down onto a pew and smiled at their group and he called them over to him.

"Eli the hero is it?" Brother Marvin asked. When Eli tried to say he was no hero the priest held up a hand. "A dragon was just singing high praises of you and I heard the bell being rung. Wear the name with pride, young man, because if your friends think you are a hero, then you are."

Eli was speechless and tried to think of a counter argument on the fly. It took a second for his brain to catch up to his words. "Don't priests usually ask people to be humble and not prideful?"

Brother Marvin slapped his knee and laughed loudly making his voice bounce off the walls. "Usually we do, but I think this is a special case that deserves it."

Bandit tugged on Eli's sleeve to get his attention and saluted him. Bandit then proudly said. "You are now Eli the hero. If you are looking to be even more official you can be my store's mascot."

George put a hand over his mouth and snickered quietly to himself as Eli stammered at the raccoon in his native tongue. The elf pulled his cloak's hood over his head and hid behind a pew as Bandit sang praises while following him around.

"Well if you boys have a moment you can pick out anything you want. After that we can get a bite to eat before we talk about the boring stuff," Brother Marvin said.

The small pile of gear got their attention and they gathered around as Brother Marvin showed off each piece. The first one was a tiny metal breastplate that fit Eli perfectly and naturally he took it. The enchanted armour would protect him from most attacks and the shiny metal matched his sword.

"This pouch can produce a dozen fruits a day. Just reach in, ask for something like an apple and one will appear in your hand," Brother Marvin said, holding a simple looking burlap sack.

"Me, me, me!" Bandit chittered, hopping up and down, reaching for the bag. "I want the snack pouch."

"Only if you share," George said firmly.

"Only the best for my friends of course," Bandit said with a wide smile.

"I think your little raccoon friend is excited," Brother Marvin said.

"He claims he will share with us, but I'm not sure if he's worthy." Eli said with an aloof tone of voice. He then broke into a big smile and nodded to the priest. "Give it to him."

Bandit was ecstatic to get the pouch and immediately tried to use it. The raccoon stuck his paws in and said. "Apple, apple, apple."

One at a time the apples came out of the bag and Bandit devoured them in rapid succession. Brother Marvin shook his head and pulled out the next time from the bag. It was a big belt and the buckle had a shiny gem set into it.

"This belt has a magic gem that will shine as brightly as the sun for a few short minutes. Pretty good to blind a monster that's on you," Brother Marvin said.

"George we can tie that to your wrist, finally a magic item you can have," Eli said.

George stuck out his arm and let Eli take a moment to tie it to his arm. Once it was secure he saw the buckle faintly glow for a second before returning to normal. Brother Marvin told him that if he tapped it three times it would activate its magic spell.

"Neat. I'll have to be careful I don't blind myself with it," George said and then looked at his scales. "Or any of you guys for that matter."

"Finally, a magic bow. Pulling on the string makes a magic arrow appear meaning you don't have to carry a quiver. The bow was blessed by the lord of the sun himself and will pierce the hide of any evil creature you encounter. If you hold the bow in front of you an arrow will hover in your free hand, showing you the way north." Brother Marvin said.

"Eli, now you can have a bow that's great at fighting evil. Now with your sword, armour and bow you can be the ultimate hero," George said.

Eli took the bow from Brother Marvin's hands reverently. The white wood bow's handle was wrapped in a piece of silk tapestry. The string was made of spun gold and when Eli plucked it, the bow made a musical ring.

"This is a rare and holy bow, are you sure you want us to have it?" Eli asked.

"Yes, and you can take this winter coat, climbing gear and tent too. The lunar temple is quite far up the nearby mountain so you will need it all. There have been tales of dangerous creatures prowling the abandoned grounds so I would rather be safe and give you as much as I can," Brother Marvin said.

They all thanked the priest for his gifts and Brother Marvin then led them towards a small house behind the grand stone church. The priest opened the door

and a feast was laid out on a huge table. Roasted
chicken, piles of fresh vegetables and garlic bread
was all on offer.

"Now, are you boys ready to have dinner?" Brother
Marvin asked.

The roar of their hungry stomachs answered for them,
and the priest laughed.

Chapter 9 - Small Court, Big Foes

The meal was fantastic, the hot food warmed their bellies and the cold juice saved them from thirst. However while Eli and Bandit enjoyed comfortable seating, George was awkwardly sitting outside and putting his head through the front door.

"I don't usually have dragon guests, so I'm very sorry I don't have the space," Brother Marivn said.

"It's alright, I'm not used to being this big either," George said.

George wiggled and got inside the cramped house by another inch. He was still within reach to eat off his plate or lap at his drink, so it didn't bother him. The only issue he would have is getting his head back out the door.

"Can you tell us more about the lunar temple?" Eli asked.

Brother Marvin ate the last piece of his pie and finished his drink. Once the priest was satisfied he leaned back into his chair and folded his hands together. The priest's brow knit together as he thought hard and after a time he seemed to know what to say.

"Long ago a group of pilgrims from the east settled high in the mountains. They traded with us and built their great stone temple in pieces. No one is sure how they made such a grand temple by themselves but it had to be with the aid of magic. Once they completed it they unveiled it to the people, showing off a diorama of the sun and planets. Soon after they vanished under the full moon, never to be seen again," Brother Marvin said.

"How is that going to help us get George to the moon?" Eli asked, he then sighed in defeat and shook his head. "Did we come all this way for nothing?"

"Some people believe the temple was a place that allowed them to walk on different planets. Perhaps there might be some clue remaining or even the chance you can find a way to talk to them," Brother Marvin said.

"It can't hurt to look around. With the wide open spaces up there I might even have room to practice flying," George said.

"Can you practice a bit closer to the ground here?" Bandit asked. He popped a berry into his mouth and looked out the window. "Those mountains would be a long fall."

"That's...a better idea," George said.

"Let's leave all this moon walking business for tomorrow. It's high time you young boys take a rest. There's plenty of room in the stable, it's full of fresh hay for you to lay on George. Eli, you could stay in a guest room here or join your friend outside." Brother Marvin said.

"I'm used to sleeping on the ground. I'll join George, if I fell asleep in a bed I would hibernate like a bear," Eli said.

Eli hopped out of his seat and thanked the priest for the gifts, the meal and for a place to rest. George repeated the gesture and Bandit gave the priest a hug. Brother Marvin yawned and thanked them all for their donation before sending the boys off to sleep.

The barn that had been offered to them was newly built, meaning that the roof was watertight and the wind couldn't blow through it. The stalls were also quite large, able to accommodate large horses for knights. George picked the biggest stall and flopped down onto the makeshift bed. His friends settled beside him, against his fire warmed side and got out their blankets.

"We are almost done with your quest George, just think, by this time tomorrow you will be back to me size," Eli said.

"Then I just need to find a way to help you, and to get home," George said.

Eli hummed to himself and curled up more into his blanket. He swatted his cat tail away, sending white fur everywhere. He sneezed from all the fur and laughed.

"I think being part cat has its merits. Maybe I should head home first before rushing into asking more magical tricksters for help," Eli said.

"You might be right," George said, thinking about the events that had led to this moment. "I'll have to be careful about my request to the dragon."

"Maybe this, maybe that, can we sleep? I need my beauty sleep," Bandit mumbled, lowering a sleeping mask onto his face. "We have to be in top shape if we are going to grab any treasure in the temple."

"No Bandit!" George and Eli shouted.

...

"Good luck storming the temple!" Brother Marvin said.

"Thank you Brother Marvin for all the help!" George shouted back.

The fresh morning was sunny and after a brief breakfast it was decided it was best to head out soon. The journey up the mountain would be long and they weren't making progress having a chat. George's talons touched the morning dew and he licked at it, tasting the sweet early rainfall.

"Time to fly?" Bandit asked.

"I can try!" George said excitedly.

He had no idea how to fly. There wasn't any new information that came to him at night, or some deep dragon insight to help. He assumed if he really wanted it he would figure it out. He only hoped it was before they were in trouble.

George made sure he was a good distance away from the church before unfurling his wings. He had seen birds run before taking off gracefully, and George figured it couldn't be that hard.

Eli and Bandit felt something off and dove off his back. George sprinted ahead, getting speed and focusing hard on flapping his wings. The results were less than fantastic. He managed to get several feet off the ground but instead of propelling himself up into the air, he instead crashed into a tree.

"George, are you okay?" Eli asked, throwing branches out of the way.

"He has a hard head, the kid is fine," Bandit said.

"Ow..." George said, holding his snout in his hands. "I don't think I have the flying part down yet."

The brief attempt to soar left a sour taste in George's mouth and not wanting to embarrass himself further he decided he would have to walk. The scenic trail was easy to hike, and the gentle slope up the mountain gradually brought them closer to their destination.

They found an open area covered in smooth slabs of rock and a raised platform on one side. The platform had carved places for people to sit but the long rectangular area was odd to him, yet familiar.

At one end of the rock slabs was a great tree with a bright orange hoop in its side, and under it was a fish net. One look around the area told George what it was for, and he started to look for the ball.

"What is this place?" Eli asked.

"It's a place to play netball," George said. "It's a fun game I played in the village where I live. My brother and I were the best around!"

The only thing off about it was the scale. The net was way too high up and when George found the ball he was taken aback by its size. It was nearly as tall as Eli was, made of interlocking black pieces and it felt odd in his hands. He gave it a bounce and felt it shoot back into his hand.

"Weird," Eli said.

Bandit leapt onto the ball and George let go, watching the raccoon bounce a few times. Once the ball settled Bandit balanced himself in the middle and stood up.

"I think this might be a ball for a giant," Bandit said.

"G-g-guys," Eli stammered.

George and Bandit looked to a frozen Eli, who pointed across to the woods. Two huge people wearing brightly coloured shirts that matched their skin walked out of the woods, one was red and one was blue. They held trees in their hands and bit off the tops of them, chewing loudly and chatting like old time friends. When the giants spotted them they dropped the trees and rushed at them.

"They are trying to steal our rubber bug!" the red giant yelled.

"Thieving dragon, get away from our stuff!" the blue giant yelled, shaking his fist.

Bandit tried to hop back onto George's back, but when his paws slipped on the slick surface he instead started to roll towards the giants. George lept towards the ball only to get smacked away by the red giant.

"Rob, you need to be careful. What if he breathes fire or turns us into squirrels?" the blue giant asked his friend.

"He won't Bob, dragons have rules they need to follow. Watch, I'll even ask," Rob the red giant said.

The red giant picked up the ball and grabbed Bandit before he could escape. When Eli tried to run the blue giant Bob took one step forward and grabbed him. George was now on his own, and flanked by two monsters as big as he was.

"You can't turn us into squirrels, right Mr. Dragon?" Rob asked.

George bit his tongue, wanting to tell the giants just what would happen if they didn't put down his friends. His mother and father always said he needed to tell the truth, and even if a lie could save his friends, he couldn't bring himself to disappoint his family.

"No," George said firmly.

"Well you go on your way, and these new folks will be our star fans for our new netball league," Bob said.

"No!" George snarled back, letting out a burst of flame. "Put them down!"

The giants recoiled in terror, with Rob holding the ball up like a weapon he wanted to throw. George wanted to push out the fire, but he only managed to cough up smoke. The giants sensing they were out of danger relaxed, and smirked at him.

"Then how about a game?" Rob asked.

"Yeah, you beat us two on one and we forget about you trespassing," Bob said.

"Trespassing?" Eli asked. He looked around the area from his high vantage point and gasped. "This is an old theatre court they turned into a place to play netball, the only people trespassing are you two."

"We found it, fair and square. Back talk to us again and I'll throw you as far as I can," Rob said, stomping his foot and shaking the ground.

The giants were getting angry and George didn't like the idea of them throwing his friends. He couldn't fly yet to save them, and it looked like the giants had a lot of muscle.

"Fine, we can play. First to three points wins. If I win, I get my friends back and an apology," George said.

"If we win, you three have to be our star fans. That means making sure we have water, handing out flyers and telling everyone we are the best," Bob said.

George hissed, but with no room to wiggle he nodded. The two giants walked over to the net and put his friends high up in the tree. With them secure in place the giants paced around the play area and pointed out the wiggly lines on the ground.

"Half-court rules, one point for a dunk, one point for a basket shot, two for a half-court shot. Two on one," Rob said.

"Fine," George said.

"I'm Bob, he's Rob," Bob said, holding out a hand.

"George, George the dragon," George said, shaking the outstretched hand.

The giants dribbled the ball to show off some moves and after making sure George knew the basic rules they tossed him the ball. The rubbery black ball felt weird in his hands and on closer inspection he saw legs between the plates.

"It's…a bug," George said.

"Rubber bug, they have really bouncy shells which make them good to play with. After the game we give it some berries and mushrooms, so it's happy to play too," Bob said.

George started dribbling the ball, feeling like he was back home playing with the other village boys. The only difference was the stakes, and he now walked around on four legs. Moving the ball was awkward at first. The giants sat back and had a smug look on their faces as he struggled. It took a minute for George to get into the rhythm but when he did, he took off like a horse, dashing between the giants.

"Rob, he's getting away," Bob said.

"Then go after him, dummy," Rob said back.

George had a lead they couldn't stop and when he reached the net he jumped high, bringing the ball down to score his first point. Only the net lurched out of the way at the last second.

"No point," The tree said.

George blinked as the tree not only moved, but spoke. In the bark he could see the vague outline of a face. Before he could react the ball was out of his clutches and Rob was running away. George sprinted to catch up only for the giant to turn after making his way to the end, signifying they were on their territory now.

"Two points!" Bob cheered.

The rubber bug sailed high into the air, out of George's reach. There was no way the wild shot could hit, but the tree twisted at the last moment, twisting its limbs to bounce the ball up into the air, and sinking it into the net.

"That's cheating!" Eli said.

"It's using your friends' help, everyone is on the court to play, so no cheating," Rob laughed.

George felt his scales shake as he restrained his anger. If the giants wanted to play that way, then he and his friends could do that too. He nodded at Eli and the elf drew his sword. It was time to use a little magic.

They reset at the end, saying they would start on George's side to help him. George dribbled the ball and hopped forwards, dipping to the side to dodge a giant's hand. He then let out a burst of smoke to obscure the area around them. He wiggled past the two colourful giants, hearing them crash together beside him.

George ran towards the tree and leapt up, leading with a claw to grab onto the moving tree. As the tree tried to shake him down he threw the rubber bug towards the net. It bounced off the rim, and Eli smacked it with the flat of his sword. The rubber bug went into the net scoring George his first point.

The giants stamped their feet and reset the field, this time on their side. George smiled and readied himself. The giants took off and as he tried to snatch the ball they threw it over his head, passing it between each other each time he almost grabbed it.

Bob readied to pass the ball and said. "Score a dunk-"

Bob slipped on a pile of marbles, his feet kicking up high into the air and sending the big man airborne. George snatched the ball and doubled back, switching back to his side. The giants had regained their feet and charged him, intent on tackling him.

George jumped onto the back of Rob, dribbled off his back and jumped again. With a flap of his wings he got extra air to dodge Bob. As he hit the ground he tossed the ball towards the net. The tree tried to swat the ball away, and from his tree tops a lightning bolt struck the branches and broke them off. The ball sunk into the net getting George his second point.

"Cheater!" Bob said, stomping his feet.

"It's using your friends' help, everyone is on the court to play after all," George said.

The court was reset again, this time for the final point. It was tense, George was at the tips of claws ready to move at the drop of a pin. The giants dribbled the ball between each other and when Rob tried to pass off George dove in to catch it. Instead Rob faked him out and tried for a two point shot.

George shot towards the ball, stretching himself out, desperate and praying he could get it. The ground disappeared from view and he heard the giants gasp behind him. George snatched the ball mid air and when he looked down to dribble it he nearly fell. He was high up in the air, or was, as he crashed back down.

The giants grabbed the ball and ran towards the net. George had no hope to catch them and watched in horror as they readied to score. An arrow made of light streaked through the air, blinding both giants and giving George the opening he needed. He grabbed the ball and brought it back, changing to his side and running for the goal. The giants squinted and tried in vain to stop the speeding orange dragon. More marbles and now apples had made their way onto the court and they were sent sprawling down onto their backsides.

George jumped, slamming the rubber bug into the net and scoring his third point. George breathed a sigh of relief, feeling the tension in the air vanish. The tree made a ringing sound and raised its branches.

"George the dragon has won," the tree said.

Eli and Bandit cheered, jumping down and running up to George. Bandit quickly ran up on George's back and slid something into the packs on his back. George could only guess what they were based on the metal sounds crashing into the bags.

The giants groaned on the ground and rose slowly while holding their backside. They settled on the platform and crossed their arms. After a tense moment they waved.

"Good game, have a good day," Rob said.

"We will just have to convince the chipmunks to be our super fans again," Bob said.

"Good luck with that," George said, gathering his friends onto his back. He grabbed the rubber bug and tossed it to them. "Here's your ball."

Rob grabbed it and from his pocket took out a berry bush. He held it out and the ball unfurled to a giant bug with too many legs. George recoiled in terror and ran off towards the mountains wanting to be away from such an odd critter.

"You flew George, I saw it, you were in the air and everything," Eli said.

"For five seconds, a glorious five seconds mind you," Bandit said.

George squared his shoulders, raising his head and smiled. "I did, let's hope I can manage five more seconds next time!"

Chapter 10 - Lunar Temple

The rest of the hike had been great. The trail had changed to a smooth, unused road. The trees gave way to open fields and the gentle slope up the mountain was easy going. However, when they reached near the top, George was dismayed.

"How are we going to get up there?" George asked.

The lunar temple wasn't near the top, it was at the very top of the mountain. The road had abruptly ended leaving rocky, sheer cliffs between them and their destination.

"Think you can fly us up there, great mighty dragon?" Bandit asked.

"If we fall… it won't end well," Eli said.

George was all about adventure and trying new things. Yet he was hesitant to try out his new wings, after all he had only managed hops so far. George shook his head and tried to look around for another way in, there had to be a path.

"There must be a secret door or something. Otherwise regular people couldn't get into the temple, so it must be near," George said.

Eli rose in the saddle and peered at the bleak rocky landscape around them. He put a hand over his eyes to block out the setting sun and when he spotted something he jumped up in excitement.

"Look over there, I can see a door carved into the cliffside," Eli said.

George couldn't see what Eli was pointing out. He followed his direction and as the cliffside got closer he noticed a disturbance in the rock. A tall stone door was outlined, barely noticeable, and had small writing around the edges.

"It's a riddle," Bandit said, hopping down and approaching the door.

I never was, am always to be. No one ever saw me, nor ever will. And yet I am the confidence of all, to live and breathe on this terrestrial ball. What am I?

George sat on his rump and coiled his tail around his talons. He hummed to himself as he tried to come up with the answer, but came up short. It was very strange, probably a secret phrase or word the lunar worshippers only knew.

"Moon, clouds, stars!" Bandit shouted. When the door didn't budge he sat beside George and got out a snack. "We might be here a while."

They took turns shouting funny phrases, or moon related things at the door. Nothing worked. Bandit kept their spirits high by handing out sandwiches or getting them drinks, but soon they ran through most of their supplies, and ideas. Hours passed and the temperature dropped rapidly, forming a light frost on the sparse grass around them.

"I think I'm stumped," Eli said in defeat.

"Same. My head hurts from all this thinking," George said.

"Well let's head back to lower ground to set up camp. It will be warmer, and we can come back tomorrow," Bandit said.

The door lit up and shifted, changing from an outline to a real door. It swung open silently, expelling dust and dry hot air that washed over them. The foreboding darkness threatened to swallow them whole.

"The answer was tomorrow… What can I say, it's a good thing you brought ol' Bandit along," Bandit said, brushing crumbs out of his fur. "I'm a professional adventurer now."

Eli held onto the bowstring and an arrow made of light appeared. It shone brightly, illuminating the area around them and giving plenty of light to see. Eli walked ahead, checking for any traps around the door while Bandit packed up lunch.

"It's safe!" Eli shouted.

Bandit finished packing up and hopped onto George's back. When George approached Eli he saw him trying to light a small lantern from his pack. The small rock and piece of steel sent out little sparks, yet the wick wouldn't light.

"We are so high up I'm not sure I can get it going," Eli said.

George leaned in and huffed towards the lantern. A little bit of fire escaped his mouth and lit the lantern's wick without a problem. Eli picked up his lantern and thanked George. With the lantern in one hand he had to switch from his bow to his sword.

"Time for some exploring," George said, bounding with excitement in his scales. "I love exploring the caves near my village."

They marched together into the mountain, walking down the long stairs made in ancient times. The air was stale and the dust was layered on so thick, George wondered how many years it had been since anyone had walked these steps.

It seemed odd that it would go down, since the temple looked to be at the mountain's peak. Perhaps there were some fancy stairs here that would head all the way to the top.

At the base of the stairs the tunnel opened up to a great chamber. It was a huge hallway that stretched forward as far as George could see. The ceiling was so far up he could see clouds and icicles forming at the top. A tiny hole in the ceiling let in a touch of moonlight, giving the entire place a dreamy feeling.

The most strange thing was the six large pillars in the hallway. They stretched from the floor to the sky, touching the ceiling at some point. There were three on each side, and it looked like the titanic blocks of stone were holding the mountain up.

In the gloom it was hard to see the details, but as Eli lifted his lantern the shapes on the pillars came to life. There were hundreds of people and creatures carved into the pillars, marching armies, monsters and high up touching the sky, dragons.

The knights on the pillars were near the bottom, riding their steeds into battle. They were so well made George thought they were real for a moment. He felt a chill run down his spine as he looked at the warhorses and saw they had fangs.

"I don't like scary horses very much, but ones with fangs are the worst," George said.

Perhaps he shouldn't have said anything. Because as George spoke the pillars began to shift. Dust floated off them and the knights began to stretch, breaking out of their stone prison and leaping down onto the path in front of them.

The mounted knights moved closer, stepping into the moonlight. Instead of being made of stone they were made of mist, and a quick glance showed the carvings were still in the pillars.

"G-g-ghost!" Eli stammered.

A thud echoed in the open chamber and when George spun around he saw a block of iron had appeared to block off the exit. With nowhere to escape, they would have to go deeper into the mountain and hope for the best.

"We can take them, watch," Bandit said.

He took out a slingshot and sent a marble straight at one of the knights. The ghostly rider raised his shield and the marble passed right through him, striking the floor and shattering apart. The knights then moved as one, rushing towards George with their weapons held high.

"Run!" Eli said, jumping onto George's back.

George sprinted to the right going around the first pillar. The knights gave chase and threw spears or shot bows towards him. Their aim was subpar and most of the attacks sailed over them or landed behind him. One knight rushed ahead of the others and swiped his sword at George's tail in a vicious arc.

George saw the attack coming in the corner of his eye and dodged at the last moment taking it out of reach of the sword. However it went near the horse and the beast bit down, ripping scales off near the end of his tail. Blood drops stained the dusty floor and George ran faster, away from the scary horse.

"Are you okay George?" Eli asked.

"Just a scrape, but feel free to shoot them!" George shouted.

His voice echoed off the walls and dislodged ancient dust. Eli handed the lantern to Bandit and took aim with his sword. He sent a lightning blast at the nearest knight, scoring a direct hit and blasted it away.

The ghost horse let out a deafening screech as it turned into dust, easing George's worries. But that small victory was short lived as the rest of the knights caught up, swarming around his sides.

George leapt into the air and unfurled his wings, getting some speed in as he glided back towards the ground. From their high vantage point he was out of the reach of most of the ghost weapons, except for the bows. Ghostly arrows bounced off his scales leaving behind strange cold sensations where they struck.

"Hold steady, I can get some of them," Eli said, readying his bow.

George twisted to avoid slamming into a pillar and managed to right himself before he lost control. Despite the dangerous blood thirsty horses trying to gobble him up, George felt relaxed as he got the hang of gliding. It wasn't really flying yet, but he was getting there.

Eli shot arrow after magic arrow, chasing the knights away. They ran far ahead, just out of their reach and waited for them. George realized he wasn't sure how to stop or get more air, which meant they were flying right into the crowd of them.

"George!" Bandit and Eli cried.

George sucked in as much air as he could. As the knights prepared to stab at him with their spears, George breathed out his fire. The wave of flames washed over the stone ground and burned away most of the ghosts in a single attack.

The warhorses ran towards him despite the flames and tried to kick with their hooves. The dragon fire ended up being too much for them and they were blasted away too, leaving a calm undisturbed hallway again.

"Look, under your feet George," Eli said.

The dragon fire had washed away years of grime, dust and goop that had settled on the floor. The hallway had carvings in the floor, running the whole length all the way to the end. It looked like grass and flowers were under his feet, under a sea of glass.

"This is amazing," George said.

He walked forwards while keeping his eyes down on the ground. The art was amazing to look at and captivated his attention. When he got near the end of where his fire had washed away the grime he felt a cold wind and looked ahead.

A bottomless pit was at the end of the walkway, a circular hole that was as wide as the hallway behind them. George leaned over and asked Eli to fire his bow. The arrow sailed down, and down, lighting up the walls until the tiny light was so far they couldn't even tell what was around it.

"Let's head back," Bandit said nervously.

George agreed and took a step back, feeling a stone shift beneath his feet and settling into the floor. A loud click rang out, bouncing off the walls of the pit, the sound echoing until it was deafening.

"Oops," George hissed.

A huge slam shook the floor and they looked behind them to see a massive boulder had crashed into the ground. The whole hallway was slightly sloped down towards the pit and when the huge rock started to move they could all tell which direction it was going to go.

"Jump?" George asked.

"Jump," Eli said grimly.

George ran to the pit just as the boulder was picking up speed. He didn't know where to go or what to do but he was going to figure out something on the fly, literally.

The stale air rushed past them and drove tears into George's eyes as he wildly looked around for an escape. The boulder crashed into the far wall and blocked out the moonlight above them. A small part of him hoped it would get stuck but the awful grinding noise meant it was coming down to chase them.

"I see the magic arrow!" Bandit said, tugging on George's horns to point him towards it. "There's something on that wall.

Eli's glowing arrow had stuck a doorway in the wall of the bottomless pit. The ancient wood was full of holes and the arrow had crashed through it easily enough. With hope in their hearts George made a dive towards it, picking up speed as he went. He crashed head first into it, splintering it apart and slammed into the floor hard.

A shadow passed behind them as the boulder continued its journey down the pit. George cracked one eye open slowly, wondering if he had really made it after all. His tired, bruised body let him know he was still breathing and George let out a tense breath he had been holding.

Eli stumbled away from the crash site and sat down onto the floor, sending dust everywhere. He ran his fingers through his hair, messing it up and rubbing dirt into his cat ears.

"Good eye Bandit, I thought we were gonners," Eli said.

"Not with good old George here to save us," Bandit said, patting George on the side. "You're getting really good at falling.

"Thanks Bandit," George wheezed.

The room they had found themselves looked like a big community dining hall. Tables and benches were all around them as far as they could see. Most were destroyed, falling apart with the passage of time but a few were more special. The ones remaining were made of rusting metal, and gave a glimpse of what must have happened here in the past.

Eli was confused and he whispered. "This is like the great dining halls elves have during festivals. Everyone dines together, the arrangement of plates, forks and knives are elvish in style too."

There were three other doors, two of which had caved in blocking the way out. The last doorway was more fine, decorated with images of plants. The ancient bronze door set into it had corroded, changing its fine artwork in a blob of greenish mess.

George rose and tried to step towards it, but his legs gave out. He crashed back onto the ground, sending dust everywhere and when the dust touched some tables, the ancient tables crumbled. It was like watching sand castles get hit with a big wave, one second there were tables, and the next, they were gone.

"George, just rest for a second. I think the ghosts hurt you," Eli said.

George didn't feel hurt, just numb in the areas he had been hit. There weren't any wounds and a tingling sensation ran down his arms. It was like the time he had slept on his arm all night, and in the morning it had taken a while before the weird feeling had passed.

Eli got out herbs, cloth and some medicine Brother Marvin had given them out of the packs. He put the mixture onto George's arms and legs and tied them with old cloth. Once George had been bandaged up he started to recover quickly.

"Brrr, it's cold down here. Good thing that priest knits for the local stray dogs," Bandit said, taking out a small scarf, hat and mittens. "I think if we find treasure here we should bring the nice guy a present."

"We shouldn't steal from a holy place, there's already ghosts crawling around," George said.

"Right, holy place and ghosts. The treasure is probably cursed anyways, so I think I'm fine leaving stuff be," Bandit said.

As Eli checked over George one more time there was a sharp clang of metal. They looked over to one of the remaining metal tables and found Bandit with an arm load of silverware.

"Bandit," George said firmly.

"George," Bandit said back in a relaxed, easy going tone.

"What did we just talk about?" George asked.

Bandit reached as far as he could and put the bundle on the edge of the table. The entire thing began to wobble and worn, rusted metal gave way. It split apart, dumping everything on the ground, making a horrendous noise.

"Bandit… why did you-" Eli stopped mid sentence and watched his breath appear in a cloud in front of him. He then started to shiver and reached for his winter gear too. "Wow it really did get cold all of a sudden."

George felt the fire inside of him heat up his limbs, giving him new strength. George spied ice forming around the bronze door and felt that was where the cold was coming from. He raised a wing and tapped Eli with it on the shoulder, getting his attention and pointing it out.

Bandit saw they were being quiet and he hushed himself. The three of them met back up and crept towards the door wondering why it was so cold. The ice had cracked the stone doorway and let through silver light.

They crowded around the door and tried to see what
was on the other side. A stone disc that could fit
George, Eli and Bandit was on the far side,
illuminated by a shaft of moonlight. In the middle was
a stone cube with a lever, George could only guess
what it was for, but Eli seemed to know.

However no one dared speak because between them
and the disc were tall towering pillars of ice. Wrapped
around each of them were giant snakes with
feathered wings, coiled around the pillars and
sleeping soundly.

They backed up to the hole they had entered in and
huddled together. The air was warmer here by quite a
margin. George was worried his friends might freeze
soon, but one look around him reminded him of all the
wood scraps.

"That's a floating disc, the elf temples back home had
them. All we have to do is reach the lever and pull it.
That moonlight must mean there's a way to the
surface, so that shaft will take us to the top," Eli said.

"What are those snake things?" George asked.

"Bad news. They are almost as big as George, and
he's huge," Bandit said firmly.

"They are bad news. Those are frost fangs, flying
poisonous snakes that can spew out ice like George

can breathe fire. They are super mean and if we wake them up then they will attack," Eli said nervously.

"Sneak past the flying danger noodles then, and we are home free," Bandit said. He pointed to the door and tried to sound encouraging. "George can do it, plus he's really good at gliding. So if we need to run he can fly us down to safety, once we reach the top."

"If we can sneak past," Eli said.

George shifted between his feet and heard his pack make a ruckus. They would have to pack everything very carefully to avoid detection. His friends got to work making sure everything in the bags couldn't rattle, creak or shift while he walked. It took a painfully long time to get it all done, but George knew that patience here was key.

Eli took out a bundle of brass coloured netball trophies and stared hard at Bandit. The raccoon shrugged and tossed them aside, removing unnecessary junk from the bags.

"Are we sure this is the best way out?" George asked.

"Unless you feel confident flying back up the giant pit," Eli said, pointing towards the bottomless pit. "I think I'll take the frost fangs over the unknown."

They were geared up, and George could see his friends suffering from the creeping cold. While he might last an account of his fire, his friends lacked it which meant they were low on time.

The wrapped pieces of worn out blankets and towels around George's claws. The strips of fabric kept the noise down and he felt more confident approaching the door. The only obstacle now was getting through.

George pushed on the door and they all collectively held their breath. The door creaked open at first, then became silent. It glided smoothly on the ice in its hinges and opened up to reveal ten sleeping frost fangs. Eli put out his lantern, meaning the only light was now moonlight, which led the way.

George crept forwards, each step tenser than the last. The cold was now getting to him, a biting monster that surrounded them all. He felt Bandit and Eli hunker down on his back, wrapped up in the remaining blankets for warmth. It seemed while his fire warmed him and his surroundings, the frost fangs chilled theirs. Worse yet, he was outnumbered ten to one when it came to changing the temperature.

George's foot stepped on something brittle, and a sharp crack broke the silence. He looked down and saw he had stepped on an ancient skeleton, reducing it to dust.

The frost fang nearest to them woke with a start and looked around. It blinked slowly as it was wondering why it had been woken up so rudely. When it saw George it was stunned, but only for a second.

"Intrudersss!" it hissed.

"Intrudersss!" the other frost fangs screeched.

Now all of them were awake and uncoiling from their sleeping spots. Not wanting to wait and explain, George decided it was time to run. He broke out in a sprint just as the monsters slammed headfirst where he had just been.

"Lightning bolt!" Eli cried, jabbing the sword forwards.

A frost fang went to block them off but ran off as lightning struck the floor near it. They had a straight shot towards the exit and George was going to take it.

"George, not to alarm you but we have a problem behind us," Bandit said.

Five of the frost fangs flew together, wing tip to wing tip and were spitting out clouds of gas. It froze the ground and left jagged pillars of ice in its wake as it got closer to them. George wasn't fast enough to escape it, so he turned on the spot.

His friends cried out in alarm but George knew what
he had to do. He reared back, puffed out his chest,
and blew out a wall of fire. The flames met the ice
breath mid air, causing steam to rise. While he was
out numbered George was still a mighty dragon. The
flames pushed back the ice and just as George ran
out of air, he won. The frost fangs had to break away,
retreating away from the ferocious dragon fire.

"The lever!" Eli cried, reminding George what he
needed to do.

George jumped and flapped his wings to get some
speed. He landed hard onto the strange stone disc
and headbutted the lever. There was a screech of
metal on metal as something clicked inside the box.
The edge of the disc glowed and the whole thing
moved up, first slowly then gaining speed.

The frost fangs made one last attempt to attack them,
but a few lightning bolts from Eli chased them away.
The disc continued to rise, and George felt his
stomach get queasy as they went faster and faster.
Just when it became too much to handle they reached
the end and the disc stopped.

Overhead was a broken stone roof letting in the star
filled sky. The moon was visible overhead, covering
the whole area in its glow. When George's eyes had
adjusted to the light he looked around and was
shocked.

They were in the gigantic mountain top temple, with huge pillars holding up the mountain's peak. His entire village could fit inside and he saw giant stone orbs hovering in the air, and at the centre was one painted bright orange.

"It's the sun," George said, recognizing what he was now seeing. "There's all the planets too."

"It's the solar system with all twelve worlds," Eli breathed.

"I don't mean to spoil the fun, but does anyone else see the dark shape standing on our planet?" Bandit whispered.

There was someone there, a big familiar someone too. George felt his scales rise, and something in the back of his head said this wasn't a friendly meeting. The dark shape unfurled its wings, jumped and flew towards them, landing a short distance away. It was the dragon he met at the lake.

Chapter 11 - Reunion

"George my boy, how is your quest coming along?" the dragon asked.

"Quite well, I just need to do one more thing," George said. "I never did catch your name back at the lake."

"You can call me, Chance," he said.

The dragon held a scroll in his claws and fanned himself with it, calling George's attention to it. It was his quest scroll and a quick look behind him showed his pack was open.

"How did you get that?" George asked.

The dragon smirked, and rolled his eyes like George should have already known the answer. The dragon stuck out his tongue and said in a mocking voice. "Just a little dash of magic, and of course luck, my name is Chance after all."

"What do you want?" Eli asked.

"What an adorable little friend you have, I've never seen such a funny looking house cat before. As for what I want, well it's simple really. I want George to take over my job," Chance said.

Eli's face reddened and he shook a fist at the huge dragon. George thought back to the first meeting with Chance. He was surprised at the time at why the red dragon had been so enthusiastic to grant him his wish, and now he knew. He still didn't understand why however.

"Do you not like the king?" George asked.

"Oh, don't get me started," Chance complained. "I'm supposed to be a lucky dragon, and I managed to get stuck in this dead end job. Ten years I've been flying messages with no vacation time. So when you asked if you could become a dragon I thought it would be great to hand over my replacement to them."

"Won't the king notice I'm a different dragon?" George asked.

"The king isn't that bright, you're big, can breathe fire, and fly. To him we are basically the same person," Chance said.

"But I need to finish my quest so I can become a boy again," George said.

Chance laughed, the sound spreading out in all directions and making the isolated chamber feel even bigger. He then opened his hand and made the scroll glow with magic. It hovered over his hand and opened up showing each line.

"The ancient hero's blade of lightning, not bad. Beat the witch at checkers? An odd achievement, but I heard her mind is sharp. Which leaves us with the last quest, sadly unfinished. If you look at the very bottom there is one other way to turn back," Chance said, hovering the scroll back over to them.

George opened the scroll all the way and saw a line that had been hidden at the very end. In tiny writing it told him that if he failed to complete the quest in one month that he would have to work as a mail dragon for ten years. Then he could earn his magic that way and choose to become a boy again.

"But my Ma said I have to turn back. If I take ten years she is going to be really mad," George said. He fell back on his rump and rubbed his head with his claws. "She is going to kill me."

"Should have read the whole thing. Can you really blame an overworked dragon?" Chance asked.

George huffed and snatched the scroll back, handing it to Bandit to put back into his bag. He glared at Chance, seeing the dragon for what he really was, a bully trying to get someone else to do his job.

"Why don't you ask the king for a vacation then, why make me do it?" George asked.

"I have tried, on many occasions, but that's not how the world works. Listen, I'm feeling generous, I can knock it down to five years if you want," Chance said, taking out the small quill George had signed the scroll with. "Just bring the scroll to me and-"

"I got it George!" Bandit said, jumping off Chance's back and grabbing the quill out of the air. "We can change the quest to something easy now!"

"You little forest thief, give that back!" Chance snarled, reaching for Bandit.

George dashed towards Bandit and slammed his shoulder into Chance's arm, knocking him away. He then picked up Bandit and had to jump out of Chance's reach as the now furious dragon had his claws out.

"Get back here, you don't know what that is capable of!" Chance growled.

Bandit crawled up George's back and got back into the saddle. Now with the magic quill all they had to do was avoid getting caught by a magical dragon twice his size. A dragon who actually knew how to fly.

Chance was already airborne and diving towards them, a speeding ball of angry snarls and claws. George ran into the giant room and felt his feet slide on icy rocks covering the ground. Chance was too close for comfort and there would be no escape on land. George swallowed his fear, jumped and flew.

"George, you're doing it. Keep it up and I'll try to keep him off us," Eli said.

"Just pass me the scroll. I'll give you a new quest, kicking this jerk's butt," Bandit said, holding the quill at the ready.

George looked down at his empty claws, and the realization hit him. He wobbled as he flew under a giant painted rock hovering in the air, what he presumed was their sister planet. He banked hard to the left, straining as the wind buffeted his wings. Chance flew over the top of the rock and shot by believing they had gone straight.

"I dropped it, we have to go back to get it," George said.

Chance figured out his deception, and in the moonlight they saw his shadow change directions. Eli brought up his bow, creating an arrow of light and sent a shot directly at the pursuing dragon. His aim was incredible and he hit Chance square in the chest, stunning the dragon for a second.

"The bow of light! Where did you ever find that?" Chance asked in bewilderment. He shook his head and continued the chase, gaining speed. "You won't stop me that easily, house cat."

"I'm an elf, Eli the hero. You better learn it fast dragon," Eli said. He sent another shot towards Chance and scowled. "You won't hurt my friends."

The arrow struck Chance's nose and made him sneeze. A burst of fire erupted in front of him and dazed him for a second. He rubbed his nose and growled in annoyance.

"Will you quit that? I'm no fiend, so your arrows only annoy me," Chance said.

"Then I'll annoy you to death if I have to," Eli said defiantly.

Arrow after arrow peppered Chance's scales keeping him at bay. George looked around wildly trying to see where he had dropped the scroll and saw it was near the stone disc that had brought them up.

"Guys, I think I see it," George said, twisting towards the scroll and got ready to dive. "Hold on tight.

George pulled his wings in and hoped for the best. He sped towards the ground with Chance hot on his tail. He was going to reach it, and then he could pass it to Bandit. He smiled already feeling his magic locked away inside him. He could fix himself, and Eli too!

A wet sensation hit his nose and he all of a sudden George felt a chill. Bandit yelped and something inside George told him there was danger. He twisted away from the disc bringing Chance with him, and it was a good thing he did too. A second later the floor exploded as the frost fangs rose into the air, hissing angrily and searching for them.

"More intrudersss, bite them all!" hissed the biggest frost fang.

The scroll was batted away from the open pit, rolling away and resting on the ground. George breathed a sigh of relief, he didn't know what would happen if the scroll was lost or destroyed, and he was hoping to never find out. Once they dealt with the frost fangs he could safely get it. That was if they could even deal with them.

The frost fangs instead of chasing him all attacked Chance. He was a bigger target and higher in the air making him more visible. The frost fangs came at him from every direction and Chance had to focus on dodging their attacks.

"We can get away, grab the scroll and run," Bandit whispered.

George frowned, Chance was being a jerk but he wasn't evil. Eli's bow didn't hurt him so that was a fact. A quick look at the battle showed that while Chance could dodge their teeth or breath fire to stop their ice, he was outnumbered. George didn't want a servant of the good king to be hurt on his watch, so they would need to save the day, like heroes.

"Bandit, start making magic happen with the quill. Eli, I'll be flying like crazy so good luck with your bow. Let's show Chance I don't need magic, I got my friends," George said.

Eli nodded in approval and looked determined to fight the frost fangs head on. Bandit however was less than enthusiastic and started to panic.

"Are you crazy, we can just leave. I don't even know how magic works, you're the dragon!" Bandit screamed.

"I don't know, write on stuff and see what happens," George said with a shrug. "You're the smartest raccoon I know, I'm sure you will figure it out."

George turned around and sped towards the nearest group of frost fangs. They didn't see him until he was almost on top of them and when he zipped by them Eli shot one square in the chest. The flash of light made the frost fang scream in pain, and the flying serpent ran away back to its pit.

"Give me some light here please," Bandit said.

Eli pulled back his bow but held the arrow in his fingers. The glowing light let Bandit see and he started to scratch down writing on the blanket he was bundled up in. Once he was done he tore off the strip and threw it.

"Here goes nothing," Bandit said, crossing his fingers.

Light exploded on the ground and the rock representing the sun glowed brightly. The entire temple shone like a beacon and magic filled the air. Bandit looked just as confused as them as the stone planets began to circle the sun, and all the icy rocks on the ground hovered into the air.

"What are you doing?" Chance shouted. "Any magic will activate the displays."

"I just wanted us to see. Sorry for trying to save your butt!" Bandit yelled back.

The battle in the temple turned into complete chaos. Display planets orbited a bright sun in the air, the icy rocks formed asteroid belts and comets shot around at blinding speeds. The moving rocky bodies however gave Chance the opening he needed to break off from the fight, and get some distance to breathe.

"Keep shooting Eli, I'll focus on keeping us in the air," George said.

"You got it," Eli said, shooting another frost fang.

"We have more problems guys," Bandit said.

George tucked his wing in and narrowly avoided a comet from smashing into his side. Once he was clear of any immediate hazards he searched for the new issue and found it quickly. The horses were back, and they were not happy.

An army of the ghost horses ran around the bottom of the temple bringing their riders towards them, and the scroll. Some had even managed to find raised platforms around the temple for watching the displays and ran off them, jumping onto planets or asteroids.

"That's just not fair," George said.

"We need that scroll George, get closer and I can get it," Bandit said, tearing off strips of the blanket. "I got more fun spells at the ready."

George's wings flapped hard and he turned to go towards the scroll, but a sense at the back of his head warned him of something coming in fast. He twisted, flying upside down and heard his friends yell as they held on for dear life. Without a second thought

George let out his fire and blocked an ice attack from two frost fangs.

"Perisssh dragon!" they hissed, bearing their fangs and trying to bite at him.

"Eli, now!" George yelled, twisting and throwing his wing out to catch one in the face.

Eli's bow shot out a dozen arrows in rapid succession, blasting the frost fangs in the face. Scorch marks dotted their icy blue scales and white feathered wings, showing each place Eli had hit. The frost fangs broke away and retreated down into the pit, deciding they weren't worth the effort.

The riders almost reached the scroll and George swooped down, knowing he was going to be late. A piece of blanket burned in the air beside him and transformed into a blazing arrow. It streaked towards the ghost riders and blasted them back into dust.

The scroll was flung high up into the air, and towards the outstretched maw of a frost fang. A massive shape collided with it, knocking the monster away. At first George thought it was a comet, but it was Chance, who grabbed the scroll and tossed it to him.

"Change the last line to something silly, anything George can do to get his magic. I used most of mine at work today and to get here," Chance said.

"I got it, I got it. Just hold steady for three seconds," Bandit said.

"Knights above us!" Eli called out.

George and Chance broke apart just as a small army of the angry horses flew past, trying to bite them with their fangs. Their ghostly riders were panicking and throwing their hands in the air as their crazy steeds threw themselves at the dragons. They fell a long way to the ground, and when they hit the rocks below they turned to dust.

"That's not steady," Bandit said.

"There's a few problems around here," George said, diving under the world. As their planet flew over their head he saw something, a small little dot in the valley by a lake. "Hey, that's my house."

"George!" Bandit cried.

"Trying," George said, trying to fly to a safe space in all the chaos.

Chance flew ahead and battered frost fangs out of the air, or breathed fire to change the direction of speeding comets. He bought them precious moments and it was all Bandit needed to scribble a line down on the scroll.

"Who's the coolest person ever?" Bandit asked.

George frowned, it was supposed to be an easy question. George felt panic set in as he saw more frost fangs come out of the pit. He twisted and said. "Oh that's a tough one, you and Eli are-"

"It's you George!" Bandit cried, holding out the scroll and tapping the new quest task with his hand. "It's you!"

"Me?" George asked in confusion. "But-"

It was good enough for the scroll. Magical golden light erupted out of the text, and a key made of light tapped George on the side. A powerful feeling passed through his limbs and a deep understanding filled him. He had magic, and plenty of it stored up too.

"Get us out of here!" Chance said, flying up beside him. "Just think of something and the magic should do the rest."

They flew past a tiny rocky planet on the outer limits of their solar system, a tiny forgettable planet. Once they rounded past it he saw their world, with the moonlight touching a familiar little dot he knew like the back of his hand. Well, his human hand that was.

"Follow me Chance. Guys, you need to hold on tight," George said.

They sped straight towards their planet, and as George focused hard, thinking about home, a small orange light appeared. It glowed at the dot and it expanded, widening and transforming into a barn door. The magical doors made of orange light opened up and the shores of the pristine lake were straight ahead.

"Portal magic? George you're a natural," Chance said.

"We just got to get there," Bandit said.

More frost fangs came at them from every side, and they were even more angry. Eli sent arrows at them, but there were just too many for him to handle on his own. Bandit threw scraps of paper, strips of blanket and even a piece of bread all with spells on them. The air around them was a sea of lightning bolts, magic arrows, dragon fire or serpent ice.

In the madness they managed to get in line with the portal and Chance tucked in his wings, gaining speed and jumping straight through. But the big frost fang came up behind the model of the moon and was coming at them from below.

"Good luck guys," George said, somersaulting in the air and grabbing his friends. Just like with netball he gave a perfect throw and banked the other way, bringing the monster with him. "Chance, catch them."

The dragon on the other side of the portal grabbed his friends out of the air and set them down. Chance began running towards him, but bounced off the barn doors. It seemed George had only managed to make it a one way portal.

"Ssstupid dragon, waking usss up. You ssshall pay for entering my lair!' hissed the big frost fang.

George was faster and more nimble than the bigger monster. He was able to fly between asteroids and other planets which forced the frost fang to go around the long way. He managed to lose him somewhere around the gas giants and flew low, hoping to avoid detection. He managed to double back and get in line with the portal, which meant he was home free.

His joy was short-lived as he saw the ghost horses without their riders running on the surface of the planet. They struck the surface of the display hard with their hooves, chipping the rock and holding onto it. Despite the portal being half way down they managed not to fall off and were gaining towards it.

George couldn't risk them getting to the village and had to do a pass, breathing fire or swiping his claws towards them. His attacks turned them to dust and it meant his village would be safe.

Stars exploded in his vision and George was tumbling through the air. With a harsh crash he slammed into their moon, knocking it out of orbit for a moment. George rose to his feet and shook his head, wondering what had happened. Standing on top of the world at the ice cap was the big frost fang, hissing and challenging him.

"You are doomed, your friendsss are gone, your portal isss gone and so isss all of your hope." It hissed.

The barn doors closed and vanished from view. The knock to his head must have broken the spell somehow, thus removing his escape. George took a step back and looked around, seeing danger everywhere. Frost fangs flew around him, more ghost knights were coming and he was alone, standing on a rock flying in the air.

"The moon, I'm standing on the moon," George said, looking down at his feet.

He twisted around and saw the scroll had gotten caught in his saddle. He grabbed it and looked again to see what Bandit had done. Bandit hadn't crossed out the third task, just added a fourth and said he only needed to get three done. As the third task glowed and the golden check mark began to form, a new line appeared. George could have one wish. George looked at his bloody claw and came up with a plan.

His foes were coming all around him and he tapped the belt's gem on his wrist three times. The light shone so brightly it was like the sun had appeared, and George closed his eyes. He heard them hiss and some of them fly away, buying him time.

He scribbled down blindly as quickly as he could, finishing the sentence just as the scroll started to vibrate. He took a breath, felt the waves of ice coming at him and heard all the arrows soaring through the air.

"I wish I was back at the beach with my friends," George said.

An orange flash, brighter than the sun erupted in the lunar temple. The unstable roof shook under the magical force and began to fall. Ancient stone which had stood the test of time finally failed, and the pillars began to topple, one after the other. To anyone who was looking at the mountain that night, it was as if the mountain top had exploded, but instead of ash and fire, it was sunlight, turning the night to day.

Chapter 12 - A Tale to Tell

A white cat walked around in a lazy circle around George's feet letting out a meow. It took a few steps away and after a flash of light stood Eli. There was a noticeable change, a lack of cat ears and tail.

"This magic ring is great. Thank you Bandit for the ring, and thanks George for putting a spell on it," Eli said.

The once simple copper ring now had a carving of a cat on its side. As Eli tapped the cat twice there was another flash of light and his ears returned. Eli knelt by the lake and smiled at his reflection, adjusting the sword at his hip before seeming satisfied.

"Friends and family discount of course. I'm just glad George turned that fairy gift into something more useful," Bandit said.

"Now I can be a cat when I want, the extra climbing skill was really helpful," Eli said.

"Well it's a good thing George the dragon could help," George said, putting his human arm around his friend.

They laughed together and high-fived. It was odd being a bit shorter than Eli, but George was glad to be normal again. Their laughter woke up the napping dragon and Chance yawned, stretching to catch the morning rays.

"Well I am glad you had the good sense to use up the rest of your magic before asking the scroll to turn you back. After we lost sight of you I thought you were a goner," Chance said.

George stretched and yawned. When he had arrived in a flash of light he was so tired he had fallen on the spot and slept all night. There was still a big depression in the ground from where he had appeared, an outline of his old dragon form.

"Well I'm glad we are all alive, but I got business to deal with. I'll be in the woods at the usual spot if you want to trade more George," Bandit said.

Bandit hopped away, his fuzzy tail vanishing into the brush behind him. George waved as his friend left and was left with a question still on his mind. He looked up to Chance and wondered how to ask the difficult question.

"There might be some after effects since you were a dragon for a good amount of time. I would assume in a few days time your animal speech will vanish. The dragon fire is probably already gone, so I don't recommend getting caught in the cold," Chance said, seemingly reading his mind.

"That's a shame," George said, shaking his head. He smacked himself and sighed. "I should have made a ring so I could talk to Bandit."

Chance smiled and looked in the direction of the capital. He hummed as he was deep in thought and then said. "When I see the king next I'll ask for a ring, I can make you that."

"Really?" George asked.

"What's the catch?" Eli asked.

Chance chuckled, the deep sound shaking the ground at their feet. He lowered his head to be at eye level with them and said. "George did save us and proved to be a very worthy dragon. I think I owe him a small favour at least."

"I'll come back to make sure you keep your promise," Eli said.

"I hope you do drop by, Eli the hero," Chance said, reaching a claw towards Eli to shake his hand.

"Good luck flying today," Eli said, shaking the mighty dragon's claw.

"You boys stay out of trouble," Chance said, dusting off his wings and preparing to take off. "Oh, and George, one more thing."

"Yes Chance?" George asked.

"Give your Ma this," Chance said, tossing the scroll to him.

George caught it mid air just as the dragon took flight. The sand of the beach was thrown everywhere, and when they could see again the dragon was gone.

George looked down at the scroll seeing it had nearly tripled in size. The quest and tasks were still there, but now there was a long line of achievements. A recounting of their journey, from saving Eli, to getting the sword. The friends they made along the way and all the perils they had succeeded against, it was quite the tale.

"Did you want to come for dinner?" George asked.

"I would love to, all that fighting last night made me really hungry and Bandit threw away all the bread," Eli said. He looked out towards the mountains and nodded. "I'll go home after, I think I need a bit of rest after all the walking."

The two of them walked back to Sleepy Hollow, chatting about their adventure and what they would do now. George had big plans to play more netball, playing with the giants had rekindled his love of sports. Eli on the other hand was going to travel and help out people, he rather enjoyed helping the merchant out.

"Someone has to help the little guys, and I don't have a big dragon to call on for help anymore," Eli said, elbowing George.

"Sorry, Ma said I had to change back. Maybe one day I'll track down Chance again and ask to be a dragon. When he saw I finished the moon task he was really confused and said the scroll was acting weird," George said.

"Yeah it was weird, when you turned back into a human there was a brief moment where I saw your shadow. It was still like you were a big dragon. Magic can do weird things," Eli said with a shrug.

They reached Sleepy Hollow and George saw what looked to be like a festival going on in the middle of town. Excitedly they ran towards it and found the entire village was together, and up on stage was the local lord, his Ma and a man in a pointy hat.

"I say, when this stick rises from my hand, it will point towards your missing boy. We need hunters to take it and go quickly to find the lad, no second chances," The man said, adjusting his hat during the speech.

It was ridiculously large, barely fitting his head and didn't even match the colour of his robes. George thought he must have been some kind of travelling wizard. The wizard hesitated to tap the stick with his magic wand, instead looking at the lord first.

"You will be paid once we find the boy," The lord said.

"Who are you looking for?" George asked, shouting towards the stage. "My friend Eli and I can help."

The crowd gasped and turned around, looking at him in shock. His Ma grabbed the stick and George saw it was her broom. Ma then shooed away the wizard with it, snacking him with the bristles. Once he was knocked away she turned and looked firmly at George.

"Where have you been, young man?" Ma asked.

George looked nervously at his furious mother, wondering what to say. Eli tapped him on the shoulder and pointed to the scroll still in his hand. George relaxed, raised the scroll high into the air and smiled proudly.

"We can fill everyone in, it's quite a tale to tell," George said. The town became quiet as everyone waited for him to speak, but cutting through the silence was his stomach that growled. George cleared his throat and said. "After lunch of course."

The next few hours rushed by as George and Eli had a quick lunch and recounted their tale, taking turns with each chapter. During the reading of the scroll Bandit came into town, and the townsfolk made sure he had a seat of honour beside the lord.

Just as Eli was reading about Bandit donating the gold to the priest he spied Bandit sliding a box towards the town sheriff. Inside it was all the lost things Bandit had been finding out in the woods for the past few years, and he quickly ran back to his seat before the guards started asking questions. Questions which would never get answered because only Eli and George could talk raccoon.

A food festival ended up happening on the spot as during each break people brought the heroes of the story hot food, cold juice or sweets to snack on to recover their strength. People even donated money to them so they could use it on travel to spread their tale, but a stern look from Ma told George that wasn't going to happen any time soon.

As the evening approached and an exhausted George read off the final words the tale was complete. The townsfolk cheered them on and the three boys in the story gathered on the stage and bowed.

Servants from the lord's house brought George, his family, Eli and Bandit to a big table. Dessert had been placed out on plates for them and George's siblings picked their favourites and started to eat.

"What's all this for?" George asked a servant.

"Cakes, gifted from the lord himself. A sign of good luck for the future and congratulations," The servant said.

The man bowed and excused himself, leaving them to enjoy their cake in peace. George slid the big slice of cake towards him. It looked fluffy and was covered in a thick layer of icing. On the top was written his name and standing in the O was a lit candle. George leaned in and tried to blow the candle out.

For a moment it vanished, turning the flickering flame into smoke. Yet for some reason it lit back up when George huffed again. He looked around the table to see everyone had already blown out their candles and were eating. So he first pinched out the fire and then blew slowly on the candle to see what would happen.

A thin line of flames shot out of his mouth relighting the candle. In the corner of his eye he could see his shadow, and something was off about it. His shadow looked a little less like George the human and a lot more like George the dragon.

"Something up?" Eli asked around a mouthful of cake.

"Nothing, just glad to be back," George said, taking a bite of the cake.

In the reflection of his silverware he saw his smile and that his teeth were a little bit sharper than normal. While his Ma might ground him for a while George thought to himself that 'George the dragon' might just soar once more.

The End